The Sea of Adventure

Enid Blyton died in 1968 at the age of seventy-one. Apart from her six hundred books – among them her well-known 'Noddy' series and 'Famous Five' novels – she wrote numerous songs, poems and plays. She also found time to run magazines and clubs at the same time.

One of the most prolific, widely read and frequently translated writers of children's books of her era, she has brought amusement and happiness to millions of children all over the world.

The sea
of adventure

Enid Blyton
Cover illustration by Juliet Stanwell-Smith
Text illustrations by Stuart Tresilian

Piccolo Pan Books
in association with Macmillan London

First published 1948 by Macmillan and Co Ltd
Abridged edition published 1969 by
William Collins Sons and Co Ltd
This Piccolo edition published 1975 by
Pan Books Ltd, Cavaye Place, London SW10 9PG,
in association with Macmillan London Ltd
8th printing 1980
Copyright Enid Blyton 1948
ISBN 0 330 24321 7
Printed in Great Britain by
Richard Clay (The Chaucer Press) Ltd, Bungay, Suffolk

Contents

Chapter 1
No governess, thank you!

'Do you know, it's May the fifth already!' said Jack, in a very gloomy voice. 'All the fellows will be back at school today.'

'What a pity, what a pity!' said Kiki the parrot, in just as gloomy a voice as Jack's.

'This awful measles!' said Lucy-Ann. 'First Philip had it as soon as he came home for the hols, then Dinah, then she gave it to me, and then you had it!'

'Well, we're all out of quarantine now,' said Dinah, from her corner of the room. 'It's just *silly* of the doctor to say we ought to go away and have a change before we go back to school. Isn't it enough change to go back to school? I do so love the summer term too.'

'Yes – and I bet I'd have been in the first eleven,' said Philip, pushing back the tuft of hair he had in front. 'Golly, I'll be glad to get my hair cut again! I feel like a girl, now it's grown so long!'

The four children had all had a bad attack of measles in the holidays. Jack especially had had a very nasty time, and Dinah's eyes had given her a lot of trouble. This was partly her own fault, for she had been forbidden to read, and had disobeyed the doctor's orders. Now her eyes kept watering, and she blinked in any bright light.

'Certainly no school work for Dinah yet,' the doctor had said, sternly. 'I suppose you thought you knew better than I did, young lady, when you disobeyed orders. Think yourself lucky if you don't have to wear glasses a little later on!'

'I hope Mother won't send us away to some awful boarding-house by the sea,' said Dinah. 'She can't come with us herself, because she's taken on some kind of important job for the summer. I hope she doesn't get us a governess or something to take us away.'

'A *governess*!' said Philip in scorn. 'I jolly well wouldn't go. And anyway she wouldn't stay now that I'm training young rats.'

His sister Dinah looked at him in disgust. Philip always had some kind of creature about him, for he had a great love of animals. He could do anything he liked with them, and Lucy-Ann secretly thought that if he met a roaring tiger in a jungle, he would simply hold out his hand, and the tiger would lick it like a dog, and purr happily like a cat.

'I've told you, Philip, that if you so much as let me *see* one of your young rats I'll scream!' Dinah said.

'All right, then scream!' said Philip obligingly. 'Hey, Squeaker, where are you?'

Squeaker appeared above the neck of Philip's jersey collar, and true to his name he squeaked loudly. Dinah screamed.

'You beast, Philip! How many of those things have you got down your neck? If we had a cat I'd give them all to her.'

'Well, we haven't,' said Philip, and poked Squeaker's head down his collar again.

'Three blind mice,' remarked Kiki the parrot, with great interest, cocking her head on one side and watching for Squeaker to appear again.

'Wrong, Kiki, old bird,' said Jack, lazily putting out a hand and pulling at his parrot's tail feathers. 'Far from being three blind mice, it's one very wide-awake rat. I say, Kiki, why didn't you catch measles from us?'

Kiki was quite prepared to have a conversation with Jack. She gave a loud cackle, and then put her head down to be scratched. 'How many times have I told you to shut the door?' she cried. 'How many times have I told you to wipe your feet? Wipe the door, shut your feet, wipe the . . .'

'Hey, you're getting muddled!' said Jack, and the others laughed. It was always comical when Kiki mixed up the things she loved to say. The parrot liked to make people laugh. She raised her head, put up her crest, and made a noise like a mowing-machine outside in the garden.

'That's enough,' said Jack, tapping her on the beak. 'Now stop it, Kiki!'

But Kiki, pleased with the noise, flew up to the top of the curtains, and went on being a mowing-machine, one that wanted oiling.

Mrs. Mannering put her head in at the door. 'Children! *Don't* let Kiki make such a noise. I'm interviewing someone, and it's very annoying.'

'Who's come for an interview?' said Philip at once. 'Mother! You haven't gone and got a governess or something awful to take us away for a change, have you? Is she here?'

'Yes, she is,' said Mrs. Mannering. All the children groaned. 'Well, dears, you know I can't spare the time to take you myself,' she went on. 'I've taken on this new job, though, of course, if I'd known you were going to be measly for so long, and then be so peaky afterwards . . .'

'We're *not* peaky!' said Philip indignantly. 'What an awful word!'

'Peaky Squeaky,' said Kiki at once, and cackled with laughter. She loved putting the same-sounding words together. 'Peaky Squeaky!'

'Shut up, Kiki!' called Jack, and threw a cushion at her. 'Aunt Allie – we can quite well go away by ourselves. We're old enough to look after ourselves perfectly.'

'Jack, as soon as I let you out of my sight in the holidays, you plunge into the middle of the most hair-raising adventures,' said Mrs. Mannering. 'I shan't forget what happened in the last summer holidays – going off in the wrong aeroplane and being lost for ages in a strange valley.'

'Oh, that was a *marvellous* adventure!' cried Philip. 'I wish we could have another. I'm fed up with being measly so long. Do, do let us go away by ourselves, Mother, there's a darling!'

'No,' said his mother. 'You're going to a perfectly safe

seaside spot with a perfectly safe governess for a perfectly safe holiday.'

'Safe, safe, safe!' shrieked Kiki. 'Sound and safe, sound and safe!'

'Other way round, Kiki,' said Jack. Mrs. Mannering put her fingers to her ears.

'That bird! I suppose I'm tired with nursing you all, but honestly Kiki gets dreadfully on my nerves just now. I shall be glad when she's gone with you.'

'I bet no governess will like Kiki,' said Jack. 'Aunt Allie, have you told her about Kiki?'

'Not yet,' admitted Mrs. Mannering. 'But I suppose I'd better bring her in and introduce her to you all and to Kiki too.'

She went out. The children scowled at one another. 'I knew it would happen. Instead of having fun at school we shall mope about with somebody we can't bear,' said Dinah gloomily. 'Phil – can't you do something with those awful rats of yours when she comes in? If she knew you were the kind of boy that likes mice and rats and beetles and hedgehogs living down his neck and in his pockets, she'd probably run for miles.'

'Jolly good idea, Dinah!' said everyone at once, and Philip beamed at her. 'It's not often you get a brainwave,' he said, 'but that's one all right. Hey, Squeaker! Come along out. Woffles, where are you? Nosey, come out of my pocket!'

Dinah retreated to the furthest corner of the room, watching the young white rats in horror. However many had Philip got? She determined not to go near him if she could possibly help it.

'I think Kiki might perform also,' said Jack, grinning. 'Kiki – puff-puff-puff!'

That was the signal for the parrot to do her famous imitation of a railway engine screeching in a tunnel. She opened her beak and swelled out her throat in delight. It wasn't often that she was begged to make this fearful noise. Lucy-

Ann put her hands to her ears.

The door opened and Mrs. Mannering came in with a tall, rather stern-looking woman. It was quite plain that no adventure, nothing unusual, would ever be allowed to happen anywhere near Miss Lawson. 'Perfectly safe' was written all over her.

'Children, this is Miss Lawson,' began Mrs. Mannering, and then her voice was drowned in Kiki's railway-engine screech. It was an even better imitation than usual, and longer drawn-out. Kiki was really letting herself go.

Miss Lawson gave a gasp and took a step backwards. At first she did not see Kiki, but looked at the children, thinking that one of them must be making the terrible noise.

'KIKI!' thundered Mrs. Mannering, really angry. 'Children, how could you let her? I'm ashamed of you!'

Kiki stopped. She put her head on one side and looked cheekily at Miss Lawson. 'Wipe your feet!' she commanded. 'Shut the door! Where's your handkerchief? How many times have I told you to . . .'

'Take Kiki out, Jack,' said Mrs. Mannering, red with annoyance. 'I'm so sorry, Miss Lawson. Kiki belongs to Jack, and she isn't usually so badly-behaved.'

'I see,' said Miss Lawson, looking very doubtful. 'I'm not very much used to parrots, Mrs. Mannering. I suppose, of course, that this bird will not come away with us? I could not be responsible for pets of that kind – and I don't think that a boarding-house . . .'

'Well, we can discuss that later,' said Mrs. Mannering hastily. 'Jack, did you hear what I said? Take Kiki out.'

'Polly, put the kettle on,' said Kiki to Miss Lawson, who took absolutely no notice at all. Kiki growled like a very fierce dog, and Miss Lawson looked startled. Jack caught the parrot, winked at the others and took Kiki out of the room.

'What a pity, what a pity!' mourned Kiki as the door shut behind them. Mrs. Mannering gave a sigh of relief.

'Jack and Lucy-Ann Trent are not my own children,' she said to Miss Lawson. 'Lucy-Ann, shake hands with Miss Lawson. Lucy-Ann and her brother are great friends of my own children, and they live with us, and all go off to boarding-school together,' she explained.

Miss Lawson looked at the green-eyed, red-haired little girl and liked her. She was very like her brother, she thought. Then she looked at Philip and Dinah, each dark-eyed and dark-haired, with a queer tuft that stuck up in front. She would make them brush it down properly, thought Miss Lawson.

Dinah came forward politely and shook hands. She thought that Miss Lawson would be very proper, very strict and very dull – but oh, so safe!

Then Philip came forward, but before he could shake hands, he clutched at his neck. Then he clutched at one leg of his shorts. Then he clapped a hand over his middle. Miss Lawson stared at him in amazement.

'Excuse me – it's only my rats,' explained Philip, and to Miss Lawson's enormous horror she saw Squeaker running round his collar, Nosey making a lump here and there over his tummy, and Woffles coming out of his sleeve. Goodness, how many more had the awful boy got!

'I'm sorry,' said Miss Lawson faintly. 'I'm very sorry – but I can't take this post, Mrs. Mannering. I really can't.'

Chapter 2
A glorious idea

After Miss Lawson had hurriedly said good-bye to Mrs. Mannering, and the front door had shut after her, Mrs. Mannering came back into the children's playroom looking very cross.

'That was too bad of you, really! I feel very annoyed and angry. How *could* you let Kiki behave like that, Jack! – and

Philip, there was no need at all for you to make those rats all appear at once.'

'But, Mother,' argued Philip, 'I can't go away without my rats, so it was only fair to let Miss Lawson know what she was in for – I mean, I was really being very honest and . . .'

'You were being most obstructive,' said Mrs. Mannering crossly. 'And you know you were. I consider you are all being really unhelpful. You know you can't go back to school yet – you all look thin and pale, and you really must pick up first – and I'm doing my best to give you a good holiday in the care of somebody responsible.'

'Sorry, Aunt Allie,' said Jack, seeing that Mrs. Mannering really was upset. 'You see – it's the kind of holiday we'd hate. We're too big to be chivvied about by Miss Lawson. Now – if it was old Bill . . .'

Old Bill! Everyone brightened up at the thought of old Bill Smugs. His real name was Cunningham, but as he had introduced himself as Bill Smugs in their very first adventure, Bill Smugs he remained. What adventures they had had with him!

'Golly, yes! – if we could go away with Bill,' said Philip, rubbing Squeaker's nose affectionately.

'Yes – and dive into the middle of another dreadful adventure,' said Mrs. Mannering. 'I know Bill!'

'Oh no, Aunt Allie – it's us children who have the adventures, and drag old Bill into them,' said Jack. 'Really it is. But we haven't heard from Bill for ages and ages.'

This was true. Bill seemed to have disappeared off the map. He hadn't answered the children's letters. Mrs. Mannering hadn't heard a word. He was not at his home and hadn't been there for weeks.

But nobody worried much about him – Bill was always on secret and dangerous missions, and disappeared for weeks at a time. Still, this time he really had been gone for ages without a word to anyone. Never mind – he would suddenly turn up, ready for a holiday, grinning all over his cheerful ruddy face.

If only he would turn up now, this very afternoon! That would be grand. Nobody would mind missing the glorious summer term for a week or two if only they could go off with Bill.

But no Bill came – and something had to be decided about this holiday. Mrs. Mannering looked at the mutinous children in despair.

'I suppose,' she said suddenly, 'I suppose you wouldn't like to go off to some place somewhere by the sea where you could study the wild sea-birds, and their nesting habits? I know Jack has always wanted to – but it has been impossible before, because you were all at school at the best time of year for it . . . and—'

'Aunt Allie!' yelled Jack, beside himself with joy. 'That's the most marvellous idea you've ever had in your life! Oh, I say . . .'

'Yes, Mother – it's gorgeous!' agreed Philip, rapping on the table to emphasise his feelings. Kiki at once rapped with her beak too.

'Come in,' she ordered solemnly, but no one took any notice. This new idea was too thrilling.

Lucy-Ann always loved to be where her brother Jack was, so she beamed too, knowing how happy Jack would be among his beloved birds. Philip too, lover of animals and birds, could hardly believe that his mother had made such a wonderful suggestion.

Only Dinah looked blue. She was not fond of wild animals, and was really scared of most of them, though she was better than she had been. She liked birds but hadn't the same interest in and love for them that the boys had. Still – to be all by themselves in some wild, lonely place by the sea – wearing old clothes – doing what they liked, picnicking every day – what joy! So Dinah began to smile too, and joined in the cheerful hullabaloo.

'Can we really go? All by ourselves?'

'When? Do say when!'

'Tomorrow! Can't we go tomorrow? Golly, I feel better just at the thought of it!'

'Mother! Whatever made you think of it? Honestly, it's wizard!'

Kiki sat on Jack's shoulder, listening to the babel of noise. The rats hidden about Philip's clothes burrowed deeply for safety, scared of such a sudden outburst of voices.

'Give me a chance to explain,' said Mrs. Mannering. 'There's an expedition setting out in two days' time for some of the lonely coasts and islands off the north of Britain. Just a few naturalists, and one boy, the son of Dr. Johns, the ornithologist.'

All the children knew what an ornithologist was – one who loved and studied birds and their ways. Philip's father had been a bird-lover. He was dead now, and the boy often wished he had known him, for he was very like him in his love for all wild creatures.

'Dr. Johns!' said Philip. 'Why – that was one of Daddy's best friends.'

'Yes,' said his mother. 'I met him last week and he was telling me about this expedition. His boy is going, and he wondered if there was any chance of you and Dinah going, Philip. You weren't at all well then, and I said no at once. But now . . .'

'But now we can!' cried Philip, giving his mother a sudden hug. 'Fancy you thinking of somebody like Miss Lawson, when you knew about this! How could you?'

'Well – it seems a long way for you to go,' said Mrs. Mannering. 'And it wasn't exactly the kind of holiday I had imagined for you. Still, if you think you'd like it, I'll ring up Dr. Johns and arrange for him to add four more to his bird-expedition if he can manage it.'

'Of course he'll be able to manage it!' cried Lucy-Ann. 'We shall be company for his boy, too, Aunt Allie. I say –

won't it be absolutely lovely to be up so far north, in this glorious early summer weather?'

The children felt happy and cheerful that teatime as they discussed the expedition. To go exploring among the northern islands, some of them only inhabited by birds! To swim and sail and walk, and watch hundreds, no, thousands of wild birds in their daily lives!...

'There'll be puffins up there,' said Jack happily. 'Thousands of them. They go there in nesting time. I've always wanted to study them, they're such comical-looking birds.'

'Puff-puff-puffin,' said Kiki at once, thinking it was an invitation to let off her railway-engine screech. But Jack stopped her sternly.

'No, Kiki. No more of that. Frighten the gulls and the cormorants, the guillemots and the puffins all you like with that awful screech when we get to them – but you are not to let it off here. It gets on Aunt Allie's nerves.'

'What a pity, what a pity!' said Kiki mournfully. 'Puff-puff, ch-ch-ch!'

'Idiot,' said Jack, and ruffled the parrot's feathers. She sidled towards him on the tea-table, and rubbed her beak against his shoulder. Then she pecked a large strawberry out of the jar of jam.

'Oh, Jack!' began Mrs. Mannering, 'you know I don't like Kiki on the table at mealtimes – and really, that's the third time she's helped herself to strawberries out of the jam.'

'Put it back, Kiki,' ordered Jack at once. But that didn't please Mrs. Mannering either. Really, she thought, it would be very very nice and peaceful when the four children and the parrot were safely off on their holiday.

The children spent a very happy evening talking about the coming holiday. The next day Jack and Philip looked out their field-glasses and cleaned them up. Jack hunted for his camera, a very fine one indeed.

'I shall take some unique pictures of the puffins,' he told Lucy-Ann. 'I hope they'll be nesting when we get there, Lucy-Ann, though I think we might be a bit too early to find eggs.'

'Do they nest in trees?' asked Lucy-Ann. 'Can you take pictures of their nests too, and the puffins sitting on them?'

Jack roared. 'Puffins don't nest in trees,' he explained. 'They nest in burrows underground.'

'Gracious!' said Lucy-Ann. 'Like rabbits!'

'Well, they even take rabbit burrows for nesting-places sometimes,' said Jack. 'It will be fun to see puffins scuttling underground to their nests. I bet they will be as tame as anything too, because on some of these bird-islands nobody has ever been known to set foot – so the birds don't know enough to fly off when people arrive.'

'You could have puffins for pets, easily, then,' said Lucy-Ann. 'I bet Philip will. I bet he'll only just have to whistle and all the puffins will come huffing and puffing to meet him.'

Everyone laughed at Lucy-Ann's comical way of putting things. 'Huffin and puffin,' said Kiki, scratching her head. 'Huffin and puffin, poor little piggy-wiggy-pig.'

'*Now* what's she talking about?' said Jack. 'Kiki, you do talk a lot of rubbish.'

'Poor little piggy-wiggy-pig,' repeated Kiki solemnly. 'Huffin and puffin, huffin and . . .'

Philip gave a shout of laughter. 'I know! She's remembered hearing the tale of the wolf and the three little pigs – don't you remember how the wolf came huffing and puffing to blow their house down? Oh, Kiki – you're a marvel!'

'She'll give the puffins something to think about,' said Dinah. 'Won't you, Kiki? They'll wonder what sort of a freak has come to visit them. Hallo – is that the telephone bell?'

'Yes,' said Jack, thrilled. 'Aunt Allie has put through a call to Dr. Johns – to tell him we'll join his expedition – but he was out, so she asked for him to ring back when he got home. I bet that's his call.'

The children crowded out into the hall, where the telephone was. Mrs. Mannering was already there. The children pressed close to her, eager to hear everything.

'Hallo!' said Mrs. Mannering. 'Is that Dr. Johns? – oh, it's Mrs. Johns. Yes, Mrs. Mannering here. What's that? Oh . . . I'm so dreadfully sorry. How terrible for you! Oh, I do so hope it isn't anything serious. Yes, yes, of course, I quite understand. He will have to put the whole thing off – till next year perhaps. Well, I *do* hope you'll have good news soon. You'll be sure to let us know, won't you? Good-bye.'

She hung up the receiver and turned to the children with a solemn face. 'I'm so sorry, children – but Dr. Johns has been in a car accident this morning – he's in hospital, so, of course, the whole expedition is off.'

Off! No bird-islands after all – no glorious carefree time in the wild seas of the north! What a terrible disappointment!

Chapter 3
Very mysterious

Everyone was upset. They were sorry for Mrs. Johns, of course, and for her husband – but as they didn't know them at all, except as old friends of Mr. Mannering long ago, the children felt far, far more miserable about their own disappointment.

'We'd talked about it such a lot – and made such plans – and got everything ready,' groaned Philip, looking sadly at the field-glasses hanging nearby in their brown leather cases. 'Now Mother will look for another Miss Lawson.'

'No, I won't,' said Mrs. Mannering. 'I'll give up my new job, and take you away myself. I can't bear to see you so disappointed, poor things.'

'No, darling Aunt Allie, you shan't do that!' said Lucy-Ann, flinging herself on Mrs. Mannering. 'We wouldn't let you. Oh dear – whatever can we do?'

Nobody knew. It seemed as if their sudden disappointment made everyone incapable of further planning. The bird-holiday or nothing, the bird-holiday or nothing – that was the thought in all the children's minds. They spent the rest of the day pottering about miserably, getting on each other's nerves. One of their sudden quarrels blew up between Philip and Dinah, and with yells and shouts they belaboured one another in a way they had not done for at least a year.

Lucy-Ann began to cry. Jack yelled angrily.

'Stop hitting Dinah, Philip. You'll hurt her!'

But Dinah could give as good as she got, and there was a loud crack as she slapped Philip full across his cheek. Philip caught her hands angrily, and she kicked him. He tripped her up, and down she went on the floor, with her brother rolling over and over too. Lucy-Ann got out of their way, still crying. Kiki flew up to the electric light, and cackled loudly. She thought Philip and Dinah were playing.

There was such a noise that nobody heard the telephone bell ringing again. Mrs. Mannering, frowning at the yells and bumps from the playroom, went to answer it. Then she suddenly appeared at the door of the playroom, her face beaming.

It changed when she saw Dinah and Philip fighting on the floor. 'Dinah! Philip! Get up at once! You ought to be ashamed of yourselves, quarrelling like this now that you are so big. I've a good mind not to tell you who that was on the telephone.'

Philip sat up, rubbing his flaming cheek. Dinah wriggled away, holding her arm. Lucy-Ann mopped her tears, and Jack scowled down at the pair on the floor.

'What a collection of bad-tempered children!' said Mrs. Mannering. Then she remembered that they all had had measles badly, and were probably feeling miserable and bad-tempered after their disappointment that day.

'Listen,' she said, more gently, 'guess who that was on the telephone.'

'Mrs. Johns, to say that Dr. Johns is all right after all,' suggested Lucy-Ann hopefully.

Mrs. Mannering shook her head. 'No – it was old Bill.'

'Bill! Hurrah! So he's turned up again at last,' cried Jack. 'Is he coming to see us?'

'Well – he was very mysterious,' said Mrs. Mannering. 'Wouldn't say who he was – just said he might pop in tonight, late – if nobody else was here. Of course I knew it was Bill. I'd know his voice anywhere.'

Quarrels and bad temper were immediately forgotten. The thought of seeing Bill again was like a tonic. 'Did you tell him we'd had measles and were all at home?' demanded Philip. 'Does he know he'll see us too?'

'No – I hadn't time to tell him anything,' said Mrs. Mannering. 'I tell you, he was most mysterious – hardly on the telephone for half a minute. Anyway, he'll be here tonight. I wonder why he didn't want to come if anyone else was here.'

'Because he doesn't want anyone to know where he is, I should think,' said Philip. 'He must be on one of his secret missions again. Mother, we can stay up to see him, can't we?'

'If he isn't later than half-past nine,' said Mrs. Mannering.

She went out of the room. The four looked at one another. 'Good old Bill,' said Philip. 'We haven't seen him for ages. Hope he comes before half-past nine.'

'Well, I jolly well shan't go to sleep till I hear him come,' said Jack. 'Wonder why he was so mysterious.'

The children expected to see Bill all the evening, and were most disappointed when no car drove up, and nobody walked up to the front door. Half-past nine came, and no Bill.

'I'm afraid you must all go to bed,' said Mrs. Mannering. 'I'm sorry – but really you all look so tired and pale. That horrid measles! I do feel so sorry that that expedition is off – it would have done you all the good in the world.'

The children went off to bed, grumbling. The girls had a bedroom at the back, and the boys at the front. Jack opened the window and looked out. It was a dark night. No car was to be heard, nor any footsteps.

'I shall listen for Bill,' he told Philip. 'I shall sit here by the window till he comes. You get into bed. I'll wake you if I hear him.'

'We'll take it in turns,' said Philip, getting into bed. 'You watch for an hour, then wake me up, and I'll watch.'

In the back bedroom the girls were already in bed. Lucy-Ann wished she could see Bill. She loved him very much – he was so safe and strong and wise. Lucy-Ann had no father or mother, and she often wished that Bill was her father. Aunt Allie was a lovely mother, and it was nice to share her with Philip and Dinah. She couldn't share their father because he was dead.

'I hope I shall keep awake and hear Bill when he comes,' she thought. But soon she was fast asleep, and so was Dinah. The clock struck half-past ten, and then eleven.

Jack awoke Philip. 'Nobody has come yet,' he said. 'Your turn to watch, Tufty. Funny that he's so late, isn't it?'

Philip sat down at the window. He yawned. He listened but he could hear nothing. And then he suddenly saw a streak of bright light as his mother, downstairs, pulled back a curtain, and the light flooded into the garden.

Philip knew what it was, of course – but he suddenly stiffened as the light struck on something pale, hidden in a bush by the front gate. The something was moved quickly back into the shadows, but Philip had guessed what it was.

'That was someone's face I saw! Somebody is hiding in the bushes by the gate. Why? It can't be Bill. He'd come right in. Then it must be somebody waiting in ambush for him. Golly!'

He slipped across to the bed and awoke Jack. He whispered to him what he had seen. Jack was out of bed and by the window at once. But he could see nothing, of course. Mrs. Mannering had drawn the curtain back over the window, and no light shone out now. The garden was in darkness.

'We must do something quickly,' said Jack. 'If Bill comes, he'll be knocked out, if that's what that man there is waiting for. Can we warn Bill? It's plain he knows there's danger for himself, or he wouldn't have been so mysterious on the telephone – and insisted he couldn't come if anyone else was here. I wish Aunt Allie would go to bed. What's the time? The clock struck eleven some time ago, I know.'

There came the sound of somebody clicking off lights and a door closing. 'It's Mother,' said Philip. 'She's not going to wait any longer. She's coming up to bed. Good! Now the house will be in darkness, and maybe that fellow will go.'

'We'll have to see that he does,' said Jack. 'Do you suppose Bill will come now, Philip? – it's getting very late.'

'If he says he will, he will,' said Philip. 'Sh—here's Mother.'

Both boys hopped into bed and pretended to be asleep.

Mrs. Mannering switched the light on, and then, seeing that both boys were apparently sound asleep, she switched it off again quickly. She did the same in the girls' room, and then went to her own room.

Philip was soon sitting by the window again, eyes and ears open for any sign of the hidden man in the bushes below. He thought he heard a faint cough.

'He's still there,' he said to Jack. 'He must have got wind of Bill coming here tonight.'

'Or more likely still, he knows that Bill is a great friend of ours, and whatever gang he belongs to has sent a man to watch in that bush every night,' said Jack. 'He's hoping that Bill will turn up sooner or later. Bill must have a lot of enemies. He's always tracking down crooks and criminals.'

'Listen,' said Philip, 'I'm going to creep out of the back door, and get through the hedge of the next-door garden, and out of their back gate, so as not to let that hidden man hear me. And I'm going up to watch for old Bill and warn him. He'll come up the road, not down, because that's the way he always comes.'

'Good idea!' said Jack. 'I'll come too.'

'No. One of us must watch to see what that man down there does,' said Philip. 'We'll have to know if he's there or not. I'll go. You stay at the window. If I find Bill coming along I'll warn him and turn him back.'

'All right,' said Jack, wishing he had the exciting job of creeping about the dark gardens to go and meet Bill. 'Give him our love – and tell him to phone us if he can, and we'll meet him somewhere safe.'

Philip slipped quietly out of the room. There was still a light in his mother's room, so he went very cautiously downstairs, anxious not to disturb her. She would be very scared if she knew about the hidden man.

He opened the back door quietly, shut it softly behind him, and went out into the dark garden. He had no torch, for he did not want to show any sign of himself at all.

He squeezed through a gap in the hedge, and came into the next-door garden. He knew it very well. He found the path, and then made his way quietly along the grass at the edge of it, afraid of making the gravel crunch a little, if he walked on it.

Then he thought he heard a sound. He stopped dead and listened. Surely there wasn't *another* man hiding somewhere? Could they be burglars, not men waiting for Bill, after all? Ought he to creep back and telephone to the police?

He listened again, straining his ears, and had a queer feeling that there was someone nearby, also listening. Listening for him, Philip, perhaps. It was not a nice thought, there in the darkness.

He took a step forward – and then suddenly someone fell on him savagely, pinned his arms behind him, and forced him on his face to the ground. Philip bit deep into the soft earth of a flower-bed, and choked. He could not even shout for help.

Chapter 4
A visit from Bill – and a great idea

Philip's captor was remarkably quiet in his movements. He had captured Philip with hardly a sound, and as the boy had not had time to utter a single cry, nobody had heard anything at all. Philip struggled frantically, for he was half choked with the soft earth that his face was buried in.

He was twisted over quickly, and a gag of some sort was put right across his mouth. His wrists, he found, were already tied together. Whatever could be happening? Did this fellow think he was Bill? But surely he knew that Bill was big and burly?

Trying to spit out the earth in his mouth behind the gag, Philip wriggled and struggled. But it was of no use, for his captor was strong and merciless.

He was picked up and carried to a summer-house, quite silently. 'And now,' hissed a voice, close to his ear, 'how many more of you are there here? Tell me that, or you'll be sorry. Grunt twice if there are more of you.'

Philip made no answer. He didn't know what to do, grunt or not grunt. Instead he groaned, for his mouth was still full of earth, and it did not taste at all nice.

His captor ran his hands over him. Then he got out a small pocket-torch, and flashed it once, very quickly, on Philip's gagged face. He saw the tuft of hair standing straight up on Philip's forehead and gave a gasp.

'Philip! You little ass! What are you doing out here, creeping about in the dark?'

With a shock of amazement and delight, Philip recognised Bill's voice. Gosh, so it was Bill! Well, he didn't mind his mouth being full of earth then. He pulled at the gag, making gurgling sounds.

'Shut up!' whispered Bill urgently, and he took off the gag. 'There may be others about. Don't make a sound. If you've anything to say whisper it right into my ear, like this.'

'Bill,' whispered Philip, his mouth finding Bill's ear, 'there's a man hidden in the bushes at our front gate. We spotted him there, and I slipped out to warn you if I could. Be careful.'

Bill undid Philip's wrists. The boy rubbed them tenderly. Bill knew how to tie people up, no doubt about that! Good thing he hadn't knocked him out.

'The back door's open,' he whispered into Bill's ear. 'As far as I know there's nobody waiting about at the back. Let's try and get into the house. We can talk there.'

Very silently the two made their way back to the gap in the hedge that Philip knew so well. Neither of them trod on the gravel, in case the slight crunch might warn any hidden watcher.

They squeezed through the gap slowly and carefully. Now they were in Philip's own garden. Taking Bill by the arm he led him slowly over the dark lawn, under the trees, towards the house. There was no light in it anywhere now. Mrs. Mannering had gone to bed.

The back door was still unlocked. Philip pushed it open, and the two of them went in. 'Don't put on the light,' whispered Bill. 'We don't want anyone to know that we're awake here. I'll lock this door.'

They went cautiously upstairs. One of the stairs creaked loudly, and Jack, who was waiting in the bedroom, shot to the door. Luckily he didn't switch the light on.

'It's all right – it's only me,' whispered Philip. 'And I've got old Bill.'

'Good egg!' said Jack in delight, and dragged them into his room. Bill gave his hand a hearty shake. He was very fond of the whole family.

'I must rinse my mouth out,' said Philip. 'It's full of earth still. I didn't dare to do any spitting out in the garden, because of the noise. Ugh! It's horrible!'

'Poor Philip!' said Bill remorsefully. 'I didn't know it was you, old fellow. I thought it was somebody lying in wait for me, and I meant to get him, before he got *me*!'

'You did it jolly well,' said Philip, rinsing his mouth out. 'Now where's my tooth-paste? I really must clean my teeth! Oh, blow!'

His hand, seeking for his tooth-paste in the dark, had knocked over a glass. It fell into the basin and smashed. It made a tremendous noise in the silent night.

'Go and warn the girls not to put their light on, if this has waked them,' said Bill urgently to Jack. 'Quick! And see if it has waked Aunt Allie. If it has, warn her too.'

Lucy-Ann was awake, and Jack just managed to stop her switching on the light. His mother did not stir. Her room was further away and she had not heard the sound of breaking glass. Lucy-Ann was astonished to hear Jack's urgent voice.

'What's up?' she asked. 'Anything gone wrong? Are you or Philip ill?'

'Of course not,' said Jack impatiently. 'Get your dressing-gown on, and wake Dinah. Bill's here! But we're not to put on any lights, see?'

Something fluttered by his head with a low squawk. 'Oh, Kiki! I wondered where you were,' said Jack. 'What made you sleep in the girls' room tonight? Come along and see Bill!'

Lucy-Ann awoke an astonished Dinah. The two girls put on their dressing-gowns and went to the boys' room. Kiki was already there, nibbling Bill's ear in delight, making soft noises in his ear.

'Hallo! hallo!' said Bill, when the girls crept softly into the room. 'Which is which? I can only feel you. Ah, this must be Lucy-Ann – I can smell your freckles!'

'You can't smell freckles,' said Lucy-Ann, giggling. 'But you're right, it is me, all the same. Oh, Bill, where have you been so long? You didn't answer any of our letters at all.'

'I know,' said Bill. 'You see – I was on a peculiar job – hunting down a gang of rogues – and then, before I knew what was happening, they got wind of what I was doing – and began to hunt *me* down! So I had to go into hiding, and keep dark.'

'Why – would they have kidnapped you or something, Bill?' asked Lucy-Ann, scared.

'Oh, there's no knowing what they would have done to me,' said Bill airily. 'I should certainly have disappeared for good. But here I am, as you see.'

'So that's what that man at the front gate was there for – hoping to get you,' said Philip. 'Why have you come to see us now, Bill? Do you want us to do anything?'

'Well,' said Bill, 'I've got to disappear for some time, and I wanted to see your mother particularly, to give her a few things to keep for me – just in case – well, just in case I didn't turn up again. I'm what is called a "marked man" now, as far as this particular gang is concerned. I know too much about them for their own comfort.'

'Oh, Bill – but where are you going to disappear to?' asked Lucy-Ann forlornly. 'I don't like you to disappear into the blue. Can't you tell us?'

'Oh – I'll probably lead the simple life somewhere in the wilds,' said Bill. 'Till these fellows have given up hunting for me, or get themselves caught. *I* don't want to disappear – don't think that! I'm not afraid of any of them, but my chiefs can't afford to let anyone get hold of me. So I've got to vanish completely for a time – and not even get into touch with you or my family.'

There was a silence. It wasn't nice to hear all this, told

in a low voice in the darkness of midnight. Lucy-Ann groped for Bill's hand. He squeezed her fingers.

'Cheer up! You'll hear from me again some day – next year, or the year after. I shall take some kind of disguise – become a miner somewhere in the wilds of Alaska – or – or a lonely ornithologist on some desolate island – or . . .'

Jack gave a gasp. Something clicked in his mind as a really brilliant idea slid into place there.

'Bill! Oh, Bill! I've thought of something grand!'

'Sh! Not so loud!' said Bill. 'And just take Kiki on your shoulder now, will you, before she nibbles away the whole of my left ear.'

'Listen, Bill,' said Jack urgently. 'I've thought of something. We had a great disappointment today – I'll tell you about it first.'

'Go on, then,' said Bill, thankful that Kiki was no longer on his shoulder.

'I don't expect you know, but we've all had measles pretty badly,' said Jack. 'That's why we're not back at school. Well, the doctor said we ought to go away for a change, and Aunt Allie decided we could go on a bird-watching expedition, with Dr. Johns and his party, to some lonely coasts and islands off the north of Britain – you know, places that only birds live on, and only bird-lovers visit.'

'I know,' said Bill, listening intently.

'Well, Dr. Johns got hurt in an accident today,' said Jack. 'So we can't go because there is nobody to take us. But – why can't *you* take us – disguised as some bird-man or other? – then we'd have a perfectly glorious holiday, you'd be able to get off into the unknown without anyone knowing – and we could leave you behind there when we come back – quite safe!'

There was silence. All the children waited breathlessly for Bill's answer. Even Kiki seemed to be listening anxiously.

'I don't know,' said Bill at last. 'It's too much like using you as a smoke-screen – and if my enemies saw through the smoke – well, things wouldn't be too good for you or for me either. I don't think it's possible.'

The mere thought of Bill's turning the wonderful idea down made the children more enthusiastic and urgent about it. They each had a few words to contribute.

'We were *so* disappointed not to go – and now this does seem a way – and after all, it would only be for about two weeks, as far as we're concerned. We'd be going back to school then.'

'You're awfully good at disguises. You could *easily* look like an ornithologist – sort of earnest, and always peering into the distance for birds, and with field-glasses over your shoulder . . .'

'Nobody could possibly know. We'd all be absolutely safe up in the northern seas, so wild and desolate, with you. Think of May up there – the sea so blue, the birds all soaring and gliding, the sea-pinks out all over the place . . .'

'You'd be *safe*, Bill – no-one surely would ever dream of hunting for you in a place like that. And oh, we do want that kind of holiday. We've felt mouldy after measles.'

'Not so *loud*,' whispered Bill. 'I'll have to talk things over with your mother first – even if I think it's all right myself. It's a bold idea – and I don't think it would occur to anyone for one moment that I would go off openly like that. And I must say that a holiday with you four – and Kiki too, of course – is just what I'm needing at the moment.'

'Oh, Bill – I believe you'll do it!' said Lucy-Ann, hugging him with ecstasy. 'What a lovely ending to a horrid day!'

Chapter 5
Exciting plans

Bill spent the night, unknown to Mrs. Mannering, in the little spare room. He said he would talk to her the next morning. He was relieved to find that a daily maid came in each morning, but that no-one except the family slept in the house at night.

'We children do all the beds and things upstairs, now that we have recovered,' said Dinah. 'So you can stay up here unseen, if you like. We'll bring breakfast up.'

But the next morning everything was upset again. Mrs. Mannering knocked on the wall separating the girls' room from hers, and Dinah went running in to see what the matter was.

'Dinah! The most sickening thing has happened!' said Mrs. Mannering in disgust. '*I've* got measles now – look at my spots. I thought I'd had it when I was your age – but it's measles right enough. Oh dear, I wish I had engaged that Miss Lawson and let her take you off to Bournemouth or somewhere yesterday. Now what are we to do?'

'Oh dear!' said Dinah. Then she decided to tell her mother about Bill being there. Perhaps that would help. 'I'll get you your dressing-jacket and tidy the room,' she said briskly, 'because there's someone who wants to see you. He may help quite a lot. It's Bill!'

'Bill!' said Mrs. Mannering, amazed. 'When did he come? I waited up till eleven, but I felt so terribly tired I just had to go to bed. Well, now – I wonder if old Bill would take you off my hands for a bit and leave Hilda, the daily, to look after me!'

'I'm sure he would,' said Dinah, delighted. 'Poor Mother! You feel worst the first two or three days and after that it's not so bad. There – are your pillows comfy? I'll send Bill in now.'

The news was broken to the others. The children were

sorry and dismayed. Did grown-ups actually get measles then? Poor Mother! Poor Aunt Allie! She would certainly want them out of the house now.

'She's ready to see you, Bill,' said Dinah. 'I say – I suppose you've had measles all right, haven't you?'

'Oh, dozens of times,' said Bill cheerfully, going to Mrs. Mannering's room. 'Cheer up – we'll get things right in no time!'

'But you can only have measles once,' began Lucy-Ann. Then the door was shut, and the children could hear only a murmur of voices in the room.

They went down to breakfast. The boys had more or less got back their ordinary appetites, but the girls still only picked at their food. Dinah looked at Lucy-Ann.

'Your freckles hardly show,' she said. 'Nor do Jack's. A bit of sun will do us all good. I don't feel like this bacon, do you? Oh dear – I wish Bill would hurry up and come down. I do want to know what they've decided.'

Bill did not come down. The children heard the door above opening, and then a soft whistle. Bill was evidently afraid the daily was about. But she had gone out to do the shopping.

'It's all right,' called Dinah. 'Hilda's out. Come down if you want to. We've saved you some breakfast.'

Bill came down. 'Your mother doesn't want any breakfast except toast and tea,' he said. 'You make the toast, Dinah. I see the kettle's boiling – we can make tea as soon as the toast is ready. Then I'm going to ring up the doctor, and then ring up Miss Tremayne, your mother's friend, and ask her to come along for a week or two to be with the invalid. She says she'll like that.'

The children listened in silence. 'And what about *us?*' asked Jack at last. 'Didn't you decide?'

'Yes, I decided,' said Bill. 'Your aunt begged me to take you away for two weeks – and I told her I was due to disappear for a while, so I'd go off to the northern seas with you. I didn't scare her with my reasons for disappearing – she's really feeling bad this morning – and she's so thankful to think you'll get away for a change that she hardly asked me any questions at all.'

'So we're to go?' said Jack, unable to keep the joy out of his voice, even though he was very sorry about Aunt Allie. 'How absolutely super!'

The four faces glowed. Kiki picked a piece of rind out of the marmalade and, as nobody said anything, took a piece of lump sugar from the sugar-basin.

'Mother will be quite all right, won't she, with Miss Tremayne?' said Philip earnestly. 'She wouldn't like one of us to stay with her, would she? I'll stay, if so.'

'She would be much better with you all out of the house,' said Bill, helping himself to bacon. 'She's tired out and wants a really peaceful time. Measles is beastly, but at least it will make her rest in bed for a while!'

'Well, then, we can really look forward to going off with a light heart,' said Jack cheerfully. 'Oh, Bill – you always turn up just exactly at the right moment!'

'Here's Hilda!' said Philip suddenly. 'You'd better hop upstairs, Bill. Take your plate. I'll bring you more toast and tea when we take Mother's up. Isn't that toast finished *yet*, Dinah?'

'Just,' said Dinah, and put the last piece in the toast-rack. 'No, Kiki, leave it alone. Oh, Jack, look at Kiki's beak – just *dripping* with marmalade. There won't be any left for us. Greedy bird!'

Bill disappeared upstairs. Hilda went into the kitchen and began to fill up the kitchen stove. Dinah went out to tell her about Mrs. Mannering having the measles. Hilda was most sympathetic, but looked very worried.

'Well, I daresay I can manage,' she said, 'but what with all you children here too . . .'

'Oh, but we shan't be,' said Dinah. 'We're going off on a bird-expedition, as soon as we can – and Miss Tremayne is coming to see to Mother – so . . .'

'Hilda! Hill-da! Hilllll-da!' called a voice, and Hilda jumped.

'My, that's the missus calling!' she said. 'And you told me she was in bed! Coming, Madam!'

But it was only Kiki, of course, doing one of her imitations. She cackled with laughter when Hilda came running into the dining-room.

'Wipe your feet!' she ordered. 'Don't sniff! How many times have I told you to . . .'

Hilda went out and banged the door. 'I don't mind taking orders from them as has the right to give them,' she said to a giggling Dinah, 'but take orders from that ridiculous bird I will not. I hope, Miss, that you're taking that parrot with you. I don't want the minding of her whilst you're gone. Drive me crazy, she would.'

'Oh, of *course* we'll take her!' said Dinah. 'Jack would never dream of going without her.'

The doctor came. Miss Tremayne arrived. Hilda agreed to sleep in. Everything seemed to be going well. Bill, ensconced in the spare room, whose door he kept locked in case Hilda should come barging in, made a few quick plans.

'Pack up your things. Order a taxi for eight o'clock tomorrow night. We'll catch the night train to the north. I'll slip out tonight and make the rest of the plans for the journey and the holiday. I'll meet you at Euston, and it won't be as the Bill Smugs you know! I shall then be Dr. Walker, the naturalist. I'll come over and introduce myself in a loud voice as soon as I see you arrive, in case there's anyone about that knows you – or me either! Then off we'll go.'

It all sounded very thrilling. What a mysterious way to begin a holiday! It sounded as if they were setting off for a first-class adventure, but of course they weren't. It would be fun if they were, but what could happen on lonely bird-islands? Nothing at all except birds, and more birds and yet more birds.

Bill slipped off that night. No one had known he was in the house, not even Miss Tremayne, who had been given the little dressing-room leading off Mrs. Mannering's room. Mrs. Mannering had promised not to say that Bill had been there, in case it meant danger to him. But she was so heavy and sleepy that day, that she really began to wonder if Bill *had* actually been there at all, or if she had dreamt it.

The children packed. No need to take best dresses or anything like that! Shorts and jerseys, rubber shoes, bathing-suits and mackintoshes were the things they would want. And a few cardigans, some towels – and what about some rugs? Were they going to sleep under a roof or not? Bill hadn't said. For all they knew they might be sleeping in tents. What fun! They decided not to take rugs. Bill would be sure to take things like that if they needed them.

'Field-glasses – note-books – pencils – my camera – and a rope,' said Jack, trying to think of everything. Lucy-Ann looked astonished.

'A *rope*?' she said. 'Why a rope?'

'We might want to go cliff-climbing if we want to examine nesting-places there,' said Jack.

'Well, you can go cliff-climbing if you like. I shan't!' said Lucy-Ann, with a shiver. 'I'd hate to climb down steep cliffs with just a rope round me and hardly anything to put my feet on.'

'Kiki's taken your pencil,' said Dinah. 'Kiki, don't be such a nuisance. We shan't take you to see the puffins if you behave like this.'

'Huffin and puffin, puffin and huffin, muffin and puffin, muffins and crumpets,' pronounced Kiki, and cracked her beak in delight at having said something new. 'Huffin and puff—'

'Oh stop huffing and puffing,' called Dinah.

'God save the King,' said Kiki, and stood up very straight.

'Goodness knows what the birds up there will think of you,' said Lucy-Ann. 'Jack, shall we put her into a basket to take her with us on the train? You know how she will keep shouting "Guard, guard" and pretending to blow a whistle, and telling everyone to wipe their feet.'

'She can go on my shoulder,' said Jack. 'We shall be sleeping on the train, in beds or berths, and she'll be quite all right. Stop cracking your beak, Kiki. It's not clever to keep *on* making a nuisance of yourself.'

'Naughty Polly!' said Kiki. 'Sing Polly-wolly-oodle-all-the-day!'

Philip threw a cushion at her and she retired to the top of the curtains and sulked. The children went on discussing their coming holiday.

'Fancy having the luck to be with Bill after all!' said Jack. 'Much better than Dr. Johns. I wonder if he'll have a boat and go exploring round. Golly, I'm going to enjoy the next week or two. We might even see a Great Auk!'

'You and your Great Auks!' said Philip. 'You know quite well they're extinct. Don't start all that again, Jack. We might find Little Auks up there, though – and razor-bills –

36

and thousands of guillemots on the cliffs.'

The next day came at last and then dragged on till the evening. Mrs. Mannering slept most of the time and Miss Tremayne would not let them go in and wake her to say good-bye.

'Better not,' she said. 'I'll say good-bye for you. Mind you write to her from wherever you're going. Is that the taxi I hear now? I'll come and see you off.'

It *was* the taxi. They bundled in with all their luggage. Now to London – to meet Dr. Walker – and to travel hundreds of miles to the north, to wild places where few people had ever been. No adventures this time, but just a glorious, carefree holiday with old Bill.

'All aboard!' said Kiki, in a deep voice that made the taxi-driver jump. 'One—two—three—OFF!'

Chapter 6
Travelling far

Bill had told the children exactly where to wait for him at Euston Station, so, each carrying a bag and a mackintosh, they went to the spot.

They stood there waiting. 'Suppose,' said Philip, in a mysterious voice, 'just suppose that one of the gang that Bill is after, knew Bill was going to meet us here – and came up and told us he was Bill – and took us all off with him, so that we were never heard of again!'

Poor Lucy-Ann stared at him in the greatest alarm. Her eyes nearly popped out of her head. 'Oh, Philip – do you think that might happen? Gracious, I hope to goodness we recognise Bill when we see him. I shall be scared stiff of going with him if we don't.'

A very fat man approached them, smiling. He was big all over, big head, big body, big feet – and big teeth that showed when he smiled. Lucy-Ann felt her heart sink. This couldn't be Bill! Nobody could make himself as big as that, if he wasn't fat to begin with. She clutched Philip's hand. Was it one of the gang?

'Little girl,' said the big man to Lucy-Ann, 'you've dropped your mackintosh behind you. You'll lose it if you don't pick it up.'

Lucy-Ann had gone pale when he first began to speak. Then she looked round and saw her mac on the ground. She picked it up. Then, scarlet in the face, she stammered out a few words of thanks.

The big man smiled again, showing all his fine teeth. 'Don't look so scared,' he said. 'I shan't eat you!'

'He looks just as if he might,' thought Lucy-Ann, retreating behind Jack.

'Pop goes the weasel,' said Kiki, in a polite conversational tone. 'Pop, pop, pop!'

'What a remarkably clever bird!' said the big man, and put out his hand to pat Kiki. She gave him a vicious nip with her beak, and then whistled like an engine.

The big man's smile vanished and he scowled. 'Dangerous bird, that,' he said, and disappeared into the crowd. The children were relieved. They didn't think, of course, that he was one of the gang – that had only been Philip's make-up – but they were worried in case he kept them talking, and prevented Bill from coming up and fetching them.

They stood there, under the clock, looking all round for Bill. They couldn't see anyone even remotely resembling him. Then a rather shambling, round-shouldered man came up, wearing thick glasses through which his eyes peered sharply.

He wore a thick long coat, had field-glasses slung across his back, and a curious black-checked cap. He also had a black beard. But he spoke in Bill's voice.

'Good evening, children. I am glad to see you are punctual. Now at last we start on our little expedition.'

Lucy-Ann beamed. That was Bill's nice warm voice all

right, in spite of the beard and the queer get-up. She was just about to fling herself on him, crying 'Oh, Bill, it's good to see you,' when Jack, feeling sure that Lucy-Ann was going to do something silly like that, pushed her away and held out his hand politely.

'Good evening, Dr. Walker. How are you?'

The others took their cue from Jack, and anyone looking on would have thought that here were four children greeting a tutor or a guardian who was going to take them on a journey somewhere.

'Come this way,' said Dr. Walker. 'I have a porter for your things. Hey, porter, put these bags on your barrow, will you, and find our reservations in the ten o'clock train. Thank you.'

It wasn't long before they were all safely on the night train. The children were thrilled with their little 'bedrooms.' Lucy-Ann liked the way everything could fold down or fold back, or be somehow pushed out of the way.

'Now, you must sleep all night,' said Bill, his eyes smiling at them from behind his thick glasses. 'Dr. Walker will see that you are awake in time for breakfast.'

'How do we get to the place we're going to, and where exactly is it?' asked Jack.

'Well, we get there by this train and another, and then by motor-boat,' said Bill. The children looked thrilled. They loved travelling.

'I've got a map here,' said Bill, making sure that the door was shut. 'It's a map of all the many little islands dotted off the north-west coast of Scotland – hundreds of them. Some are too small to map. I don't expect anyone has ever visited all of them – only the birds live there. I thought we'd make one of them our headquarters, and then cruise around a bit, taking photographs, and watching the birds in their daily life.'

The eyes of the two boys gleamed. What a glorious thing to do! They visualised days of sunshine on the water, chugging to and from tiny islands inhabited by half-tame birds, picnicking hungrily in the breeze, sitting on rocks with their feet dangling in the clear water. Their hearts lifted in happiness at the thought.

'What I should really like,' said Philip, 'would be a tame puffin or two. I've never seen a live puffin – only a stuffed one – but they look real characters.'

'I suppose you would teach them to sit up and beg,' said Bill, amused.

'Huffin and puffin,' announced Kiki. 'God save the King.'

Nobody took any notice. They were all too much absorbed in thinking of their unusual holiday.

'I shall remain behind there, once you have gone back,' said Bill. 'It'll be a bit lonely without you all, but no doubt you will leave me your tame puffins for company.'

'I shall hate leaving you,' said Lucy-Ann. 'Will you have to be there all alone for long, Bill?'

'A goodish time, I expect,' said Bill. 'Long enough for my enemies to forget about me, or to think I'm dead and gone.'

'Oh dear!' said Lucy-Ann. 'I wish you didn't have to lead such a dangerous life, Bill. Can't you do something else instead?'

'What? Be a gardener, or a tram conductor or something safe like that, do you mean?' asked Bill, grinning at Lucy-Ann's serious face. 'No, Lucy-Ann – this kind of life suits me. I'm on the side of law and order and right – and to my mind they're worth while running any risk for. Evil is strong and powerful, but I'm strong and powerful too, and it's good to try one's strength against bad men and their ways.'

'Well, I think you're marvellous,' said Lucy-Ann stoutly. 'And I'm sure you'll always win. Don't you hate having to hide now?'

'I'm furious about it,' said Bill, looking anything but furious, but with a note in his voice that made the others realise how desperate he felt, having to 'disappear' when there was work to be done. 'But – orders are orders. And anyway, my disappearance means a perfectly glorious holiday for all of us. Well, boys, have you finished studying that map?'

The two boys had been poring over the map of islands. Jack put his finger on one. 'Look – that sounds a good one – the Isle of Wings – it must be full of birds!'

'We'll try and go there,' said Bill. 'We shall probably get well and truly lost, but never mind. Who minds being lost on the blue-green sea in May-time, with all kinds of little enchanted islands ready to welcome you?'

'It sounds glorious,' said Dinah. 'Oh, look at Kiki. She's trying to pull the plug off its chain in that basin.'

Kiki had thoroughly explored the whole of the 'bedroom,' and had had a good drink out of one of the water decanters. Now she settled down on the little towel-rail and, with a remarkably human yawn, put her head under her wing. At the same moment there came a loud banging of doors all down the train. She took her head out again.

'Shut the door,' she remarked. 'Pop goes the door. Send for the doctor.'

The whistle blew, and to Kiki's alarm the whole 'bedroom' suddenly shook as the train pulled out of the station. She almost fell off the towel-rail.

'Poor Kiki, what a pity, what a pity!' she said, and flew to Jack's shoulder.

'Now it's time we all retired to bed and to sleep,' said Bill, getting up. He looked very queer in his black beard and thick glasses. Thank goodness he had taken off the awful black-checked cap.

'Do two of us sleep here, or four of us?' asked Lucy-Ann, looking doubtfully at the small beds, one on each side of the 'bedroom.'

'Two, silly,' said Bill. 'I've got a single room on the right of you – and to the right again is another compartment, or

41

room, for the two boys. I'm in the middle of you, you see – and you've only to bang hard on the wooden wall between us, if you want anything, and I'll come rushing in.'

'Oh, good!' said Lucy-Ann. 'I'm glad you're so near us. Bill, are you going to sleep in your beard?'

'Well, as it's rather painful to remove at the moment, being well and truly stuck on, I think I will,' said Bill. 'I'll take it off when we're safely among our little islands. No one will see us there. Don't you like me in my beautiful beard?'

'Not much,' said Lucy-Ann. 'I feel as if you're not you when I look at you, but when I hear your voice, it's all right.'

'Well, my child, look at me with your eyes shut, and you'll have no horrid feelings,' said Bill, with a grin. 'Now good night, and sleep well. Come on, boys, I'll take you to your compartment. I'll wake you in the morning, and we'll dress and go along to the restaurant car for breakfast.'

'I feel a bit hungry now,' said Philip, 'although we had a jolly good supper. But that's ages ago.'

'Well, I've got some sandwiches and some bananas,' said Bill. 'I'll get them. But don't be long turning in, because it's getting late.'

'Only just gone ten,' said Dinah, but she yawned loudly as she spoke. Kiki promptly imitated her, and that set everyone else yawning too.

Bill went into his own compartment and fetched sandwiches and ripe bananas. Then he said good-night to the girls and took the boys to their own 'bedroom.' It really was very exciting to go to bed in a train. It was queer undressing with the train swaying about, rushing through the night at sixty miles an hour.

It was nice to be in bed, listening to the 'tutta-tut-*tah!* tutta-tut-*tah!*' of the train wheels turning rapidly over the rails.

'Travelling *far*, travelling *far*, travelling *far*,' said the wheels to Lucy-Ann, as her eyes closed, and her mind swung towards sleep. 'Travelling *far* . . .'

In spite of all the excitement the four children were soon fast asleep and dreaming. What were they dreaming of? That was easy to guess. Blue-green water, clear as crystal, enchanting little islands, big white clouds flying across an enormous blue sky, and birds, birds, birds . . . travelling *far*, travelling *far*, travelling *far*.

Chapter 7
On the sea at last

The journey was half over before the children awoke again. Bill banged on the walls, and they woke with a jump. They dressed and walked staggeringly along to the restaurant car, feeling very hungry. Lucy-Ann didn't much like walking across the bits that joined two carriages together. She clutched Bill's hand then.

'I'm always afraid the train might come in two, just when I'm walking through the bit where two carriages are joined,' she explained. Bill quite understood, and didn't even smile, though the others were very scornful of Lucy-Ann's extraordinary idea.

Kiki behaved very badly at breakfast, throwing the toast about, and squawking because she was not allowed any of the rather small helping of marmalade. She made rude noises at the sunflower seeds Jack offered her. The other passengers were amused at her and laughed – but that only made Kiki show off all the more.

'Stop it, Kiki,' said Bill, exasperated, and tapped her smartly on the beak. Kiki screeched and made a pounce at his beard. A vicious tug and some of it came away. Kiki hadn't been able to understand why Bill had arrived with a strange mass of hair under his chin, and round his cheeks. Now, having got some of it, she retired under the table and

began to peck it gently, separating the hairs one by one and murmuring to herself all the time.

'Let her be,' said Bill. 'She'll be happy pulling that bit of my beard to pieces.' He rubbed his chin. 'That hurt. I hope I don't look too peculiar now?'

'Oh no – it doesn't really show much,' Jack assured him. 'Kiki always gets excited on a journey like this. She's awful when I bring her back from school – whistles like the guard, and tells all the people in the carriage to blow their noses and wipe their feet, and screeches in the tunnels till we're almost deafened.'

'But she's a darling really,' said Lucy-Ann loyally, and didn't say a word about Kiki undoing her shoe-laces and pulling them out of her shoes at that very moment!

The journey was a long one. There was a change to be made at a very big and noisy station. The next train was not quite so long as the first one and did not go so fast. It took them to a place on the coast, and the children were delighted to see the blue sea shining like a thin bright line in the distance. Hurrah! They all loved the sea.

'Now I feel that our holiday has really begun,' said Lucy-Ann. 'Now that we've seen the sea, I mean. It gives me a proper holiday feeling.'

Everyone felt the same, even Kiki, who leapt about like a Red Indian doing a war-dance, on the luggage-rack above the children's heads. She flew down to Jack's shoulder when they got out of the train at a big seaside town.

The strong breeze blew in their faces, and the girls' hair streamed back. Bill's beard blew back too, and Kiki was careful to stand with her beak to the wind. She hated her feathers being ruffled the wrong way.

They had a very good meal in a hotel, and then Bill went down to the harbour to see if his motor-boat was there. It had just come in. The man who brought it knew Bill very well, and had been told in what disguise he was to be seen.

'Morning, Dr. Walker, sir,' he said in loud tones. 'Fine

weather for your expedition. Everything's ready, sir.'

'Plenty of provisions, Henty?' asked Dr. Walker, blinking through his thick glasses.

'Enough to stand a siege, sir,' said Henty. 'I'm to pilot you out, sir – I've got a boat behind.'

Everyone went on board. It was a fine motor-boat, with a little cabin in front. Jack's eyes gleamed when he saw the stock of food – tins, tins, tins! The little refrigerator was full of stuff too. Good! There would be plenty to eat anyway, and that, in Jack's opinion, was one of the main things to be planned for, on a holiday. People always got so terribly hungry when they were holidaying.

Henty piloted them out of the harbour, his tiny boat bobbing about. When they were beyond the harbour Henty saluted and got into his boat.

'Well – good luck, sir,' he said. 'The wireless is O.K., sir – we'll be expecting a message regularly, to know you're all right. There are extra batteries, and a repair set as well. Good luck, sir. I'll be here in two weeks' time to pick up the kids.'

He rowed off, his oars making a soft plash-plash-plash in the water. He soon looked very small indeed, as Bill's motor-boat sped away.

'Well – we're off!' said Bill, with great satisfaction. 'And my beard can come off too – and my glasses, thank goodness. And my coat. Here, Philip, you know how to steer a motor-boat, don't you? Take the wheel whilst I make myself presentable again. No one is likely to see me now. Keep her going north-north-west.'

Proudly Philip took the wheel. The engine of the boat purred smoothly, and they sped fast over the blue water. It was a wonderful day, almost as hot as summer. The May sun shone down out of a sky flecked with tiny curly clouds, and little points of light danced on the waves.

'Gorgeous!' said Jack, sitting down with a grunt of joy near Philip. 'Simply absolutely perfectly gorgeous.'

'I've got such a lovely feeling,' said Lucy-Ann, looking the picture of happiness. 'You know – that feeling you get at the very beginning of a lovely holiday – when all the days spread out before you, sunny and lazy and sort of enchanted.'

'You'll end up by being a poet if you don't look out,' said Philip, from the wheel.

'Well, if a poet feels like I feel just exactly at this moment, I wouldn't mind being one for the rest of my life, even if it meant having to write poetry,' said Lucy-Ann.

'Three blind mice, see how they run,' remarked Kiki, and for one moment everyone thought that Kiki was joining in the talk about poetry, and giving what she thought was an example. But she was merely referring to the three tame rats that had suddenly appeared on Philip's shoulders. They stood there daintily, their pink noses raised, sniffing the salt sea air.

'Oh, blow you, Philip!' said Dinah, from her seat near Jack. 'I was hoping against hope you hadn't brought those detestable little creatures. I only hope the gulls eat them.'

But even Dinah couldn't feel annoyed for long as they glided over the green waves, leaving a white wake behind them, like a long feathery tail. When Bill appeared from the little cabin, they all hailed him in delight.

'Bill! Dear old Bill, you look like yourself again!'

'Oh, Bill – never wear a beard again. It does spoil your beauty.'

'Hurrah! We've lost Dr. Walker for ever. Silly fellow, I never liked him.'

'Bill, you look nice again. I can see your mouth when you smile.'

'Pay the bill, pay the bill!'

'Shut up, Kiki, or the gulls will get you!'

'Ah, this is something like,' said Bill happily, taking the wheel from Philip. 'Golly, if we get this weather we'll all be burnt black in a day or two. Better keep your shirts on, boys, or you'll get blistered.'

Everyone had discarded coats and wraps at once. The breeze was cool, but the sun was really very hot. The sea, in the distance, was unbelievably blue, the colour of cornflowers, Lucy-Ann thought.

'Now, my friends,' said Bill, his white shirt billowing in the breeze, 'this is a holiday, not a hair-raising adventure. You've had enough of adventures. We've had three together, and this time I want a holiday.'

'Right,' said Jack. 'A holiday it shall be. Adventures keep out!'

'I don't want any adventures either,' said Lucy-Ann. 'I've had plenty. This is adventure enough for me. I like this kind best – not the kind where we have to hide, and creep through secret tunnels and live in caves. I just want a sunny, lazy, windy time with the people I like best. It would be nice if Aunt Allie was here too – but perhaps she wouldn't enjoy it very much.'

'I hope she's feeling better,' said Dinah. 'I say, where's the land? I can't see a bit – not even an island!'

'You'll see plenty tomorrow,' said Bill. 'You can choose one for your own.'

That was a wonderful afternoon and evening. They had a fine tea on board, prepared by the two girls, who found new bread, strawberry jam and a big chocolate cake in the cabin larder.

'Make the most of this,' said Bill. 'You won't get new bread often now. I doubt if we shall find any farmhouses at all, among the lonely islands we shall visit. But I've brought tins and tins of biscuits of all kinds. And as for this chocolate cake, eat it up and enjoy it – I don't think you'll get any more for two weeks.'

'I don't care,' said Dinah, munching away. 'When I'm hungry I simply don't mind *what* I eat – and I can see I'm always going to be hungry on this holiday.'

The sun went down in a great golden blaze, and the tiny curly clouds turned a brilliant pink. Still the motor-boat went on and on and on, over a sea that blazed pink and gold too.

'The sun has drowned itself in the sea,' said Lucy-Ann at last, as it disappeared. 'I watched the very very last little bit go down into the water.'

'Where are we going to sleep tonight?' asked Jack. 'Not that I mind – but it would be fun to know.'

'There are two tents somewhere in the bow,' said Bill. 'I thought, when we came to an island we liked the look of, we'd land, put up the tents and sleep there for the night. What do you say?'

'Oh *yes*,' said everyone. 'Let's look for an island – a really nice wild one!'

But at the moment there was no land in sight, not even a small rocky island. Bill gave the wheel to Jack, and looked at the chart. He pointed with his finger. 'We've been running in this direction. We should come on these two islands presently. One has a few people on it, and, I believe, a tiny jetty. We'd better go there tonight, and then set off to the unknown tomorrow. It's getting too late to go hunting for islands further away. It would be dark before we got there.'

'It's still very light,' said Philip, looking at his watch. 'At home it would be getting dark.'

'The further north you go, the longer the evening light is,' said Bill. 'Don't ask me why at the moment. I don't feel capable of a lecture just now.'

'You don't *need* to tell us,' said Philip loftily. 'We learnt all about it last term. You see, owing to the sun being . . .'

'Spare me, spare me,' begged Bill, taking the wheel again. 'Look, one of your inquisitive little rats is sniffing at Kiki's tail. There will be murder done in a moment if you don't remove him.'

But Kiki knew better than to hurt any of Philip's pets. She contented herself with cracking her beak so loudly in Squeaker's ear that he ran back to Philip in alarm, scampering up his bare legs and into his shorts in a trice.

Gradually the sea lost its blue, and became grey-green. The breeze felt cold and everyone put on jerseys. Then far away in the distance a dark hump loomed up – land!

'That's it, that's one of the islands we want for tonight,' said Bill, pleased. 'I consider I've done pretty well to head so straight for it. We'll soon be there.'

It certainly was not long before they were nosing alongside a simple stone jetty. A fisherman was there, in a long blue jersey. He was astonished to see them.

Bill explained in a few words. 'Och, so it's bairds ye're after,' said the fisherman. 'Weel, there's plenty for you out yon,' and he nodded towards the sea. 'Where will you be sleeping the night? My bit cottage won't tak' sae mony.'

Lucy-Ann couldn't understand him, but the others gathered what he meant. 'Bring the tents,' ordered Bill.

'We'll soon have them up. We'll get the fisherman's wife to give us a meal. It will save our own provisions. Maybe we can get some cream too, and good butter.'

By the time that darkness came at last they had all had a good meal, and were bedded down in the two tents, comfortable on ground-sheets and rugs. The fresh air had made them so sleepy that the girls fell asleep without even saying goodnight.

'They're a' daft,' said the fisherman to his wife. 'Wasting a fine boat like yon, looking for bairds. *Bairds!* When there's good fish to be got! Well, they'll soon see bairds in plenty. Och, they're a' dafties!'

Chapter 8
The island of birds

Next day, after a fine breakfast of porridge and cream, and grilled herrings, the tents were struck and the five went aboard their boat. It was called *Lucky Star*, which the children thought was a very nice name.

Kiki had not been popular with the old fisherman and his wife. They had never seen a parrot before, and they could not understand a bird that talked. They regarded Kiki with awe and fear, and seemed scared of her sharp, curved beak.

'God save the King,' said Kiki, having learnt by experience that most people thought this was a fine thing for her to say. But she spoilt it by adding. 'Pop goes the King, pop, pop, pop!'

Now she was aboard with the others, and once again the boat was skimming over the blue water. Once again the sky was blue and the sun was hot. True May weather, that made the sea a clear, translucent blue, and set thousands of little sparkles dancing over the water.

'I've still got that lovely feeling,' said Lucy-Ann happily, as she dangled her hand over the side of the boat and felt the cool, silky water catch hold of her fingers and trail them back. 'Now to find some bird-islands. We really are going to find some today, aren't we, Bill?'

'We certainly are,' said Bill, and gave the boat a little extra speed. Spray came up and fell lightly over everyone.

'Ooooh, lovely!' said Dinah. 'I was so hot. That cooled me beautifully. Let her out again, Bill! I could do with some more of that.'

For five hours they sped over the water, and then Jack gave a shout. 'The islands! Look, you can see little blobs here and there on the horizon! They must be the islands!'

And now the children began to see a great many different birds on the water and in the air. Jack called out their names excitedly. 'There's a shearwater! Jolly good name for it. And look, Philip, that's a razorbill! – and gosh, is that a Little Auk?'

The boys, well versed in the appearance of the wild sea-birds, almost fell overboard in their excitement. Many of the birds seemed to have no fear of the noisy boat at all, but went bobbing on their way, hardly bothering to swerve when it neared them.

'There's a shag diving,' shouted Jack. 'Look! you can see it swimming under water – it's caught a fish. Here it comes. It's clumsy getting out of the water to fly. Gosh, if only I'd got my camera ready!'

Kiki watched the many birds out of baleful eyes. She did not like the interest that Jack suddenly appeared to take in these other birds. When a great gull appeared, flying leisurely right over the boat, Kiki shot up underneath it, gave a fearful screech, and turned a somersault in the air. The gull, startled, rose vertically on its strong wings and let out an alarmed cry.

'EEE-oo-ee-ooooo!'

Kiki imitated it perfectly, and the gull, thinking that Kiki must be some strange kind of relation, circled round. Then it made a pounce at the parrot. But Kiki flipped round, and then dropped to Jack's shoulder.

'Eee-oo!' she called defiantly, and the gull, after a doubtful glance, went on its way, wondering, no doubt, what kind of a gull this was that behaved in such a peculiar manner.

'You're an idiot, Kiki,' said Jack. 'One of these days a gull will eat you for his dinner.'

'Poor old Kiki,' said the parrot, and gave a realistic groan. Bill laughed. 'I can't imagine what Kiki will do when we see the puffins, waddling about among the heather and sea-pinks,' he said. 'I'm afraid she will give them an awful time.'

As they came nearer to the first island, more and more birds were to be seen on and above the water. They glided gracefully on the wind, they dived down for fish, they bobbed along like toy ducks. There was a chorus of different cries, some shrill, some guttural, some mournful and forlorn. They gave the children a wild, exultant kind of feeling.

As they came near to the island the children fell silent. A tall cliff towered in front of them, and it was covered from top to bottom with birds! The children stared in delight.

Birds, birds, birds! On every ledge they stood or squatted, thousands of white gannets, myriads of the browner guille-mots, and a mixture of other sea-birds that the boys could hardly make out, though they glued their field-glasses to their eyes for minutes on end.

'What a coming and going!' said Bill, staring with fascinated eyes, too. And it certainly was. Besides the birds that stood on the ledges, there were always others arriving and others leaving. That way and this went the busy birds, with a chorus of excited cries.

'They're not very careful with their eggs,' said Lucy-Ann, in distress, when she looked through Jack's glasses in her turn. The careless birds took off and knocked their precious eggs over the ledge and down the cliff, to be smashed on the rocks below.

'They can lay plenty more,' said Philip. 'Come on, Lucy-Ann – give me back my glasses! Golly, what a wonderful sight! I shall write this all up in my notes tonight.'

The motor-boat nosed carefully round the rocky cliffs. Bill stopped looking at the birds and kept a sharp look-out instead for rocks. Once round the steep cliffs the land sloped downwards, and Bill spotted a place that seemed suitable for the boat.

It was a little sheltered sandy cove. He ran the boat in and it grounded softly. He sprang out with the boys, and made it safe, by running the anchor well up the beach and digging it in.

'Is this going to be our headquarters?' asked Dinah, looking round.

'Oh, *no*,' said Jack at once. 'We want to cruise round a bit, don't we, Bill, and find a puffin island. I'd really like to be in the *midst* of the bird-islands, and be able to go from one to the other as we pleased. But we could stay here for tonight, couldn't we?'

That was a wonderful day for the four children, and for Bill too. With thousands of birds screaming round their heads, but apparently not in the least afraid of them, the children made their way to the steep cliffs they had seen from the other side of the island.

Birds were nesting on the ground, and it was difficult to tread sometimes, without disturbing sitting birds or squashing eggs. Some of the birds made vicious jabs at the children's legs, but nobody was touched. It was just a threatening gesture, nothing more.

Kiki was rather silent. She sat on Jack's shoulder, her head hunched into her neck. So many birds at once seemed to overwhelm her. But Jack knew that she would soon recover, and startle the surrounding birds by telling them to wipe their feet and shut the door.

They reached the top of the cliffs, and were almost deafened by the cries and calls around them. Birds rose and fell in the air, glided and soared, weaving endless patterns in the blue sky.

'It's funny they never bump into one another,' said Lucy-Ann, astonished. 'There's never a single collision. I've been watching.'

'Probably got a traffic policeman,' said Philip solemnly. 'For all you know some of them may have licences under their wings.'

'Don't be silly,' said Lucy-Ann. 'All the same, it *is* clever of them not to collide, when there's so many thousands. What a row! I can hardly hear myself speak.'

They came to the very edge of the cliff. Bill took Lucy-Ann's arm. 'Not too near,' he said. 'The cliffs are almost sheer here.'

They were. When the children lay down on their tummies and looked cautiously over, it gave them a queer feeling to see the sea so very very far below, moving slowly in and out, with only a far-off rumble to mark the breaking of the waves. Lucy-Ann found herself clutching the cushions of sea-pink beside her.

'I somehow feel I'm not safe on the ground,' she said with a laugh. 'I feel as if I've got to hold on. I feel sort of – well, sort of upside-down!'

Bill held on to her tightly after that speech. He knew that she felt giddy, and he wasn't going to risk anything with little Lucy-Ann! He liked all the children very much, but Lucy-Ann was his favourite.

The children watched the birds going and coming endlessly to and from the narrow cliff ledges. It was a marvellous sight. Jack looked through his glasses and chuckled at the squabbling and pushing that was going on, on some of the narrower shelves.

'Just like naughty children,' he said. 'Telling each other to move up and make room, or I'll push you off – and off somebody goes, sure enough. But it doesn't matter, because out go their wings and they have a lovely glide through the air. My word, I wouldn't mind being a sea-bird – able to stride along on the sea-shore, or bob on the sea, or dive for

fish, or glide for miles on the strong breeze. I shouldn't mind be—'

'What's that?' said Philip suddenly, hearing a noise that wasn't made by sea-birds. 'Listen! An aeroplane, surely!'

They all listened, straining their eyes through the sun-washed air. And, far away, they saw a speck, steadily moving through the sky, and heard the *r-r-r-r* of an engine.

'A plane! Right off all the routes!' said Bill. 'Well – that's the last thing I expected to see here!'

Chapter 9
Hurrah for Puffin Island!

Bill seemed so astonished that the children stared at him. Surely it wasn't so surprising to see an aeroplane, even near these desolate bird-islands?

Bill took Jack's glasses and looked through them, but it was too late to make out anything.

'I wonder if it was a seaplane or an ordinary plane,' he said, half to himself. 'Queer.'

'Why is it queer?' asked Dinah. 'Aeroplanes go everywhere now.'

Bill said no more. He handed back the glasses to Jack. 'I think we'd better have a meal, and then put up our tents,' he said. 'What about putting them by that little stream we saw on our way here? About a quarter of a mile from the shore. It wouldn't be too far to carry everything if we all give a hand.'

The tents were set up. The ground-sheets were put down and the rugs tumbled over them. Then, sitting on a slight slope, looking out to the blue sea, the five of them had a glorious meal. 'I always think,' began Lucy-Ann, munching a couple of biscuits with butter and cream cheese between them. 'I always think . . .'

'You needn't go on,' said Jack. 'We know what you're

going to say and we quite agree with you.'

'You *don't* know what I'm going to say,' said Lucy-Ann indignantly.

'We do,' said Philip. 'You say it every holiday when we have a meal out of doors.'

'You're going to say, "I always think food tastes *much* nicer when it's eaten out of doors," ' said Dinah. 'Aren't you?'

'Well, I was,' said Lucy-Ann. 'Do I really always say it? Anyway, it's quite true. I *do* think . . .'

'Yes, we know,' said Jack. 'You're an awful repeater, Lucy-Ann. You tell us the same things over and over again. Never mind. We think the same, even if we don't keep on saying it. Kiki, take your fat beak out of the cream cheese!'

'Kiki's awful,' said Dinah. 'She really is. She's pinched three biscuits already. I don't think you give her enough sunflower seeds, Jack.'

'Golly, I like *that*!' said Jack. 'She won't even *look* at sunflower seeds when there's a spread like this. Anyway, Philip, your rats can always eat them. I found Squeaker in my pocket a little while ago, nibbling one of them as fast as he could.'

'I hope it won't make him ill,' said Philip in alarm. 'I say, look! – here comes a gull – tame as anything. It wants a biscuit too, I should think.'

It did. It had watched Kiki pecking at a biscuit and enjoying it, and it didn't see why it shouldn't have a share. Kiki saw the gull out of the corner of her eye and sidled away. The gull made a pounce, got the biscuit and rose into the air, making a loud laughing noise. 'Ee-oo, ee-oo, ee-oo!'

Kiki flew up angrily, calling out all kinds of things to the gull. They were meant to be very rude, but unfortunately the gull didn't understand. Kiki could not catch the strong-winged bird and flew disconsolately back to the children.

'You can't complain, Kiki,' said Jack. 'You shouldn't have pinched that biscuit out of the tin – and the gull shouldn't have pinched it from you. It's six of one and half a dozen of the other.'

'What a pity, what a pity!' said Kiki, and sidled near the biscuit-tin again.

'That bird is a real clown,' said Bill, shaking the crumbs off his jersey. 'Now, who's coming back to the boat with me to hear the news on the wireless? Also I must send out a few messages – especially one for your mother, Philip, who will be sure to want to know if we've got here safely.'

They all wanted to stretch their legs, so they walked back over the soft cushions of the sea-pinks, whose bold little pink heads nodded everywhere in the wind.

They watched Bill as he put up his little wireless mast and fiddled about with the set. It was a transmitter as well as a receiver.

'I suppose if you send messages home every night, we shan't need to post letters off to Aunt Allie,' said Lucy-Ann.

Everyone roared. 'And where would you post a letter, pray?' asked Jack. '*I* haven't seen a pillar-box anywhere about. Lucy-Ann, you're an idiot.'

'Yes, I am!' said Lucy-Ann, going red. 'Of course we can't post anything here! How useful that you can send messages, Bill! Then if any of us wanted help, you could get it.'

'Quite so,' said Bill. 'But I hope if you wanted help I could whizz you off in the motor-boat. Anyway I wouldn't have consented to bring you all away into the wilds like this, if I hadn't a transmitter with me, so that I could send messages every night. I send them to headquarters, and they telephone them to your aunt. So she'll follow our travels and adventures each night.'

They watched for a while, and then listened to part of a programme. Then Lucy-Ann yawned and Kiki imitated her. 'Blow! You make me feel sleepy,' said Dinah, rubbing her eyes. 'Look, it's getting dark!'

So back they went to their tents, and were soon cuddled

into their rugs. The birds called incessantly from the cliffs and the sea. 'I believe they keep awake all night,' thought Dinah. But they didn't. They slept too when the darkness came at last.

The next day was very warm and close. 'Looks to me like a storm blowing up sooner or later,' said Bill, screwing up his eyes and looking into the bright sky. 'I almost think we'd better try and find our headquarters today, so that we have some shelter if a storm does blow up. This sort of holiday needs fine weather if it's going to be successful – a storm wouldn't be at all pleasant, with only tents to sleep in – we'd be blown to bits.'

'I just want to take a few photographs of these cliffs and the birds on them,' said Jack. 'I'll do that whilst you're getting down the tents, if you don't mind my not helping you.'

So off he went with Kiki towards the steep cliffs. Bill called after him that he was not to try any climbing down the cliffs, and he shouted back that he wouldn't.

Soon everything was packed away again on the motor-boat, which was just being floated by the rising tide, and they waited patiently for Jack. He soon appeared, his glasses and his camera slung round his neck, and his face beaming.

'Got some beauties,' he said. 'Kiki was awfully useful to me. I got her to parade up and down, so that all the birds stayed still in amazement, watching her – and then, click! I got them beautifully. I ought to have some fine pictures.'

'Good!' said Bill, smiling at the enthusiastic boy. 'You'll have to have a book of bird photographs published. "*Masterpieces*, by Jack Trent, price thirty shillings."'

'I'd like that,' said Jack, his face shining. 'Not the thirty shillings I mean – but having a book about birds with my name on it.'

'Come on in,' said Philip impatiently, for Jack was still outside the boat. 'We want to be off. It's so warm I'm longing to get out to sea again, and feel the breeze on my face as the boat swings along.'

They soon felt it and were glad of it. It certainly was very hot for May. The boat went swiftly through the water, bobbing a little as it rode over the waves. Lucy-Ann let her fingers run through the water again – lovely and cool!

'What I should like is a bathe,' said Philip, little drops of perspiration appearing round his nose. 'Can we bathe from the boat, Bill?'

'Wait till we get to another island,' said Bill. 'I don't particularly want to stop out at sea, with a storm in the offing. It's so jolly hot I feel there must be thunder about. I'm anxious to run for shelter before it comes. Now – here are more islands bobbing up out of the sea. Let's see if we can spot a puffin island. That's what you want, isn't it?'

Lucy-Ann, still dangling her hand in the water, suddenly felt something gently touching it. In surprise she looked down, withdrawing her hand at once, afraid of a jellyfish.

To her astonishment she saw that it was a piece of orange peel, bobbing away on the waves. She called to Bill.

'Bill, look – there's a bit of orange peel. Now whoever in the world eats oranges in these wild little islands? Do you suppose there are any other bird-lovers somewhere about?'

Everyone looked at the tiny bit of orange peel bobbing rapidly away. It did seem very much out of place there. Bill stared at it hard. He was puzzled. The fishermen, if there were any on the islands they were coming to, would not be at all likely to have oranges. And naturalists surely would not bother to load themselves up with them.

Then how did that bit of peel come to be there? No ships went anywhere near where they were. It was a wild and lonely part of the sea, where sudden storms blew up, and great gales made enormous waves.

'Beats me!' said Bill at last. 'I shall expect to see a pine-apple or something next! Now look! – here is an island – fairly flattish – probably has puffins on it all right. Shall we make for it?'

'No – cruise round a bit,' begged Jack. 'Let's have a look

at a few of the islands here. There is quite a colony of them round about.'

They cruised round, looking at first this island and then that. They came to one that had steep cliffs at the east side, then ran down into a kind of valley, then up again into cliffs.

Jack put his glasses to his eyes and yelled out excitedly. 'Puffins! Plenty of them! Can you see them, Philip? I bet the island is full of their burrows. Let's land here, Bill. There'll be masses of birds on the cliffs, and hundreds of puffins inland. It's quite a big island. We could probably find good shelter here and water too. The cliffs would protect us from both the east and west. What ho, for Puffin Island!'

'Right,' said Bill. He looked all round and about, and guided the boat towards the island. There were many other islands not far off, but as far as he could see they were inhabited only by birds. The sea chopped about between the islands, making little rippling waves.

Round Puffin Island went the boat, and Philip gave a shout. 'Here's a fine place to put the boat in, Bill – see, where that channel of water goes into a cleft of the cliff! It'll be deep there, and we can just tie the boat up to a rock. We'll put out the fenders, so that she doesn't bump against the rock sides.'

The boat nosed into the channel. As Philip said, the water was deep there – it was a natural little harbour. There was a ledge of rock on which they could land. Could anything be better? Hurrah for Puffin Island!

Chapter 10
A little exploring

'Isn't this a gorgeous place?' said Jack, as the boat glided gently into the little channel. There was just room for it. 'It might be a boat-house made specially for the *Lucky Star*.'

Bill leapt out on to the rocky ledge, which did very well for a landing-stage. Sheer above them on each side rose rocky cliffs. Rows and rows of birds sat on the ledges, and there was a continual dropping of eggs, knocked off by the careless birds. One broke near Bill, and splashed its yellow yolk over his foot.

'Good shot!' he yelled up to the circling birds, and the children roared.

They made the boat fast by tying the mooring-rope round a convenient rock. The boat bobbed up and down gently as waves ran up the little channel and back.

'Tide's up now,' said Bill. 'When it goes down there will still be plenty of water in this channel. The boat will look much lower down then. Now – is there a way up the cliff from here? We don't want to have to walk down the ledge and clamber round the cliffs over hundreds of rocks before we get on to the island proper.'

They looked round. Jack ran up the rocky ledge, and then turned and gave a shout. 'Hi! We can get up here, I think. There are rocky shelves, like rough steps, going up the cliff – and there's a break in it a bit above. We could probably clamber out all right, and find ourselves right on the island.'

'Well, you four go and explore,' said Bill. 'I'd better stay with the boat and see that she doesn't get her sides smashed in against these rocks. You look round the island and see if you can spot a sheltered cove somewhere, that I can take the boat round to.'

The children left the boat and followed Jack. Kiki flew

on ahead, calling like a gull. Up the rocky ledges went Jack. They were almost like giant steps, roughly hewn by the great wintry seas for century after century.

As Jack said, the cliff had a deep cleft in it just there, and the children found that they could make their way through it, and come out on to the cushions of sea-pinks beyond. It needed a bit of clambering, and they were out of breath when they reached the top – but it was worth it.

The sea spread bright blue all round the island. The sky looked enormous. Other islands, blue in the distance, loomed up everywhere. A real colony of them, it seemed – and their island was in the centre.

Then Jack gave such a yell that everyone jumped. 'Puffins! Look! Hundreds and hundreds of them!'

The children looked to where Jack pointed, and there, among the sea-pinks and the old heather tufts, were the most curious-looking birds they had ever seen.

They were dressed in black and white. Their legs were orange – but it was their extraordinary bills that held the children's attention.

'Look at their beaks!' cried Dinah, laughing. 'Blue at the base – and then striped red and yellow!'

'But what *enormous* beaks!' cried Lucy-Ann. 'They remind me a bit of Kiki's.'

'Puffins are called sea parrots,' remarked Jack, amused to see the crowd of solemn-looking puffins.

'Their eyes are so comical,' said Philip. 'They stare at us with such a fixed expression! And look at the way they walk – so upright!'

The colony of puffins was as good as a pantomine to watch. There were hundreds, thousands of birds there. Some stood about, watching, their crimson-ringed eyes fixed seriously on their neighbours. Others walked about, rolling from side to side like a sailor. Some took off like small aeroplanes, eager to get to the sea.

'Look! – what's that one doing?' asked Lucy-Ann, as a

puffin began to scrape vigorously at the soil, sending a shower of it backwards.

'It's digging a burrow, I should think,' said Dinah. 'They nest underground, don't they, Jack?'

'Rather! I bet this island is almost undermined with their holes and burrows,' said Jack, walking forward towards the colony of busy birds. 'Come on – do let's get near to them. Kiki, keep on my shoulder. I won't have you screaming like a railway engine at them, and scaring them all away.'

Kiki was most interested in the comical puffins. She imitated their call exactly. 'Arrrrr!' they said, in deep guttural voices. 'Arrrrrrrr!'

'Arrrrrr!' answered Kiki at once, and various birds looked up at her enquiringly.

To the children's huge delight the puffins were not in the least afraid of them. They did not even walk away when the children went near. They allowed them to walk among them, and although one aimed a peck at Philip's leg when he stumbled and almost fell on top of it, not one of the others attempted to jab with their great beaks.

'This is lovely!' said Lucy-Ann, standing and gazing at the extraordinary birds. 'Simply lovely! I never thought birds could be so tame.'

'They're not exactly tame,' said Jack. 'They're wild, but they are so little used to human beings that they have no fear of us at all.'

The puffins were all among the cushions of bright sea-pinks. As the children walked along, their feet sometimes sank right down through the soil. The burrows were just below, and their weight caused the earth to give way.

'It's absolutely mined with their burrows,' said Philip. 'And I say – it's not a very nice smell just about here, is it?'

It certainly wasn't. The boys soon got used to it, but the girls didn't like it. 'Pooh!' said Lucy-Ann, wrinkling up her nose. 'It's getting worse and worse. I vote we don't put our tents up too near this colony of puffins – it's as bad as being near a pig-sty.'

'Don't make a fuss,' said Jack. 'Hey, come here, Kiki!'

But Kiki had flown down to make friends. The puffins gazed at her fixedly and solemnly.

'Arrrr!' said Kiki politely. 'ARRRRRRRR! God save the King!'

'Arrrr!' replied a puffin, and walked up to Kiki, rolling from side to side like a small sailor. The two looked at one another.

'I shall expect Kiki to say how-do-you-do in a minute,' said Dinah, with a little squeal of laughter. 'They both look so polite.'

'Polly put the kettle on,' said Kiki.

'Arrrr!' said the puffin, and waddled off to its hole. Kiki followed – but apparently there was another puffin down the hole, who did not want Kiki's company, for there was soon an agonised squeal from the parrot, who shot out of the hole much more rapidly than she had gone in.

She flew up to Jack's shoulder. 'Poor Kiki, what a pity, what a pity, what a pity!'

'Well, you shouldn't poke your nose in everywhere,' said Jack, and took a step forward. He trod on a tuft of sea-pinks, which immediately gave way, and he found his leg going down into quite a deep burrow. Whoever lived in it didn't like his leg at all, and gave a vicious nip.

'Ooooch!' said Jack, sitting down suddenly and rubbing his leg. 'Look at that – nearly had a bit right out of my calf!'

They went on through the amazing puffin colony. There were puffins on the ground, in the air – and on the sea too! 'Arrrr! Arrrr! Arrrr!' their deep calls sounded every-where.

'I'll be able to take some magnificent photographs,' said Jack happily. 'It's a pity it's too early for young ones to be about. I don't expect there are any puffin eggs yet either.'

The puffins were living mainly in the green valley between the two high cliffs. Philip looked about to see if there was any good place to pitch their tents.

'I suppose we all want to make Puffin Island our head-quarters?' he said. 'I imagine that nothing will drag Jack away from here now. He's got cliffs where guillemots and gannets nest, and a valley where the puffins live – so I suppose he's happy.'

'Oh *yes*,' said Jack. 'We'll stay here. This shall be *our* island – we'll share it with the puffins.'

'Well, we'll find a good place for our tents,' said Philip. 'Then we'll bring our goods and chattels here and camp. We'd better find a place where there's a stream, though . . . if there *is* one on this island. We shall want water to drink. And let's look for a cover where we can put the boat. We can't very well leave it in that narrow channel.'

'Look – there's a dear little cove down there!' said Dinah suddenly, pointing to the sea. 'We could bathe there – and the boat would be quite all right there too. Let's go and tell Bill.'

'I'll go,' said Philip. 'Jack wants to stare at the puffins a bit more, I can see. I'll take the boat round to the cove with Bill, and you two girls can find a good place for our tents. Then we'll all help to bring the things there from the boat.'

He ran off quickly to find Bill and tell him where to put the boat. Jack sat down with Kiki to watch the puffins. The girls went to look for a good place to put up their tents for the night.

They wandered over the island. Beyond the puffin colony, just at the end of it, before they came to the high cliffs at the other side of the island, was a little dell. A few stunted birch-trees grew there, and banks of heather.

'This is just the place,' said Dinah, pleased. 'We can put up our tents here, be sheltered from the worst of the wind, watch the puffins, go down to bathe when we want to, and when we're tired of that, go cruising round the other islands.'

'A very nice life,' said Lucy-Ann, with a laugh. 'Now – is there any water about?'

There was no stream at all on the island – but Dinah found something that would do equally well. At least, she hoped it would.

'Look here!' she called to Lucy-Ann. 'Here's an enormous rock with a hollow in its middle, filled with water. I've tasted it and it isn't salt.'

Lucy-Ann came up, followed by Jack. Dinah dipped in her hand, scooped up a palmful of water and drank. It was as sweet and as pure as could be.

'Rain-water,' said Dinah pleased. 'Now we'll be all right – so long as it doesn't dry up in this hot weather. Come on – let's go back to the boat and collect all the things we want. We'll have to do a bit of hard work now.'

'We'll wait here a bit,' said Jack, coming up with Kiki. 'I expect Bill and Philip will be bringing the boat round to the cove over there – then we'll go and tell them we've found a good place, and help to bring the things here.'

It was not long before Bill and Philip ran into the cove with the boat. Bill leapt out, took the anchor well up the beach and dug it in. He saw Jack and the girls and waved to them.

'Just coming!' he cried. 'Have you found a good place for the tents?'

He and Philip soon joined the others, and were pleased with the little dell. 'Just right!' said Bill. 'Well, we'll bring all the things we want from the boat straight away now.'

So they spent quite a time going to and from the cove, laden with goods. It did not take quite as long as they feared because there were five of them to do it, and even Kiki gave a hand – or rather a beak – and carried a tent-peg. She did it really to impress the watching puffins, who stared at her seriously as she flew by, the peg in her big curved beak.

'Arrrrrr!' she called, in a puffin voice.

'You're showing off, Kiki,' said Jack severely. 'You're a conceited bird.'

'Arrrrr!' said Kiki, and dropped the tent-peg on Jack's head.

It was fun arranging their new home. The boys and Bill were to have one tent. The girls were to have the other. Behind the tents Lucy-Ann found a ledge of rock and below it was a very large dry space.

'Just the spot for storing everything in,' said Lucy-Ann proudly. 'Jack, bring the tins here – and the extra clothes – there's room for heaps of things. Oh, we *are* going to have a lovely time here!'

Chapter 11
Huffin and Puffin

'Isn't it about time we had a meal?' complained Jack, staggering over with a great pile of things in his arms. 'It makes my mouth water to read "Spam" and "Best Tinned Peaches" and see that milk chocolate.'

Bill looked at his watch and then at the sun. 'My word – it certainly is time! The sun is setting already! How the time has flown!'

It wasn't long before they were all sitting peacefully on tufts of sea-pink and heather, munching biscuits and potted meat, and looking forward to a plate of tinned peaches each. Bill had brought bottles of ginger-beer from the boat, and these were voted better than boiling a kettle to make tea or cocoa. It was very warm indeed.

'I feel so happy,' said Lucy-Ann, looking over the island to the deep-blue sea beyond. 'I feel so very very far away from everywhere – honestly I hardly believe there is such a thing as school, just at this very minute. And this potted meat tastes heavenly.'

Philip's white rats also thought it did. They came out

from his clothes at once when they smelt the food. One sat daintily upright on his knee, nibbling. Another took his tit-bit into a dark pocket. The third perched on Philip's shoulder.

'You tickle the lobe of my ear,' said Philip. Dinah moved as far from him as she could, but, like Lucy-Ann, she was too happy to find fault with anything just then.

They all ate hungrily, Bill too, their eyes fixed on the setting sun and the gold-splashed sea, which was now losing its blue, and taking on sunset colours. Lucy-Ann glanced at Bill.

'Do you like disappearing, Bill?' she asked. 'Don't you think it's fun?'

'Well – for a fortnight, yes,' said Bill, 'but I'm not looking forward to living in these wild islands all alone, once you've gone. It's not my idea of fun. I'd rather live dangerously than like one of these puffins here.'

'Poor Bill,' said Dinah, thinking of him left by himself, with only books to read, and the wireless, and nobody to talk to.

'I'll leave you my rats, if you like,' offered Philip generously.

'No, thanks,' said Bill promptly. 'I know your rats! They'd have umpteen babies, and by the time I left this would be Rat Island, not Puffin Island. Besides, I'm not so much in love with the rat-and-mouse tribe as you are.'

'Oh, look, do look!' suddenly said Dinah. Everyone looked. A puffin had left its nearby burrow and was walking solemnly towards them, rolling a little from side to side, as all the puffins did when they walked. 'It's come for its supper!'

'Then sing, puffin, sing!' commanded Jack. 'Sing for your supper!'

'Arrrrrrr!' said the puffin deeply. Everyone laughed. The puffin advanced right up to Philip. It stood close against the boy's knee and looked at him fixedly.

'Philip's spell is working again,' said Lucy-Ann enviously. 'Philip, what makes all animals and birds want you to be friends with them? Just look at that puffin – it's going all goofy over you.'

'Don't know,' said Philip, pleased with his queer new friend. He stroked the bird's head softly, and the puffin gave a little *arrrrr* of pleasure. Then Philip gave it a bit of potted-meat sandwich and the bird tossed it off at once and turned for more.

'Now I suppose you'll be followed round by a devoted puffin,' said Dinah. 'Well, a puffin is better than three rats, any day – or mice – or that awful hedgehog with fleas that you had – or that pair of stag-beetles – or . . .'

'Spare us, Dinah, spare us,' begged Bill. 'We all know that Philip is a walking zoo. Personally, if he likes a goofy puffin, he can have it. I don't mind a bit. It's a pity we haven't brought a collar and lead.'

The puffin said 'Arrrr' again, a little more loudly, and then walked off, perfectly upright, its brilliant beak gleaming in the setting sun.

'Well, you didn't pay us a very long visit, old thing,' said Philip, quite disappointed. The puffin disappeared into its burrow – but reappeared again almost immediately with another puffin, a little smaller, but with an even more brilliant beak.

'Darby and Joan!' said Jack. The two birds waddled side by side to Philip. The children looked at them in delighted amusement.

'What shall we call them?' said Dinah. 'If they are going to join our little company, they'll have to have names. Funny little puffins!'

'Huffin and puffin, huffin and puffin,' remarked Kiki, remembering the words suddenly. 'Huffin and . . .'

'Yes, of course – Huffin and Puffin!' cried Lucy-Ann in delight. 'Clever old bird, Kiki! You've been talking about Huffin and Puffin ever since we started out on our holiday –

72

and here they are, Huffin and Puffin, as large as life!'

Everyone laughed. Huffin and Puffin did seem to be perfectly lovely names for the two birds. They came close to Philip, and, to the boy's amusement, squatted down by him contentedly.

Kiki was not too pleased. She eyed them with her head on one side. They stared back at her with their crimson-ringed eyes. Kiki looked away and yawned.

'They've out-stared Kiki!' said Jack. 'It takes a lot to do that!'

The three rats had prudently decided that it was best to keep as far away from Huffin and Puffin as possible. They sat round Philip's neck, gazing down at the two birds. Then, at a movement from Huffin, they shot down the boy's shirt.

Bill stretched himself. 'Well, I don't know about you kids – but I'm tired,' he said. 'The sun is already dipping itself into the west. Let's clear up, and turn in. We'll have a lovely day tomorrow, bathing and sunning ourselves, and watching the birds. I'm getting used to their eternal chorus of cries now. At first I was almost deafened.'

The girls cleared up. Lucy-Ann dipped a bowl into the clear pool of water and handed it round for washing in. 'We oughtn't to wash in that pool, ought we, Bill?' she said seriously.

'Good gracious, no!' said Bill. 'It would be absolutely black after the boys had gone in! We'll keep it for drinking-water only, or just take our water from it when we want it for boiling or washing.'

'I think I'll go and have a dip now,' said Jack, getting up. 'No, not in the rock-pool, Lucy-Ann, so don't look so upset – I'll go down to the little cove where the boat is. Coming, Philip?'

'Right,' said Philip, and pushed Huffin and Puffin away from his knees. 'Move up, you! I'm not growing here!'

'I'll come too,' said Bill, and knocked out the pipe he had been smoking. 'I feel dirty. You girls want to come?'

'No,' said Lucy-Ann. 'I'll get the rugs and things ready for you in the tents.'

Dinah didn't want to go either, for she felt very tired. Measles had certainly taken some of the energy out of the two girls. They stayed behind whilst the others set off to the cove to bathe. The valley sloped right down to the sea just there, and the small sandy cove was just right for bathing. The boys and Bill threw off their things and plunged into the sea. It felt lovely and warm, and rippled over their limbs like silk.

'Lovely!' said Bill, and began to chase the boys. With howls and yells and splashings they eluded him, making such a terriffic noise that Huffin and Puffin, who had solemnly accompanied Philip all the way, half walking and half flying, retreated a little way up the beach. They stared at the boys fixedly and thoughtfully. Philip saw them and was pleased. Surely nobody had ever had two puffins for pets before!

The girls were setting out ground-sheets and rugs neatly in the two tents when Dinah suddenly stopped and listened. Lucy-Ann listened too.

'What is it?' she whispered – and then she heard the noise herself. An aeroplane again, surely!

The girls went out of the tent and looked all over the sky, trying to locate the sound. 'There! – there, look!' cried Lucy-Ann excitedly, and she pointed westwards. 'Can't you see it? Oh, Dinah – what's it doing?'

Dinah couldn't spot the plane. She tried and tried but she could not see the point in the sky where the aeroplane flew.

'Something's falling out of it,' said Lucy-Ann, straining her eyes. 'Oh, where are the boys' field-glasses? Quick, get them, Dinah!'

Dinah couldn't find them. Lucy-Ann stood watching the sky, her eyes screwed up.

'Something dropped slowly from it,' she said. 'Something white. I saw it. Whatever could it have been? I hope the aeroplane wasn't in any trouble.'

'Bill will know,' said Dinah. 'I expect he and the boys saw it all right. Maybe they took the glasses with them. I couldn't find them anywhere.'

Soon there was no more to be seen or heard of the plane, and the girls went on with their work. The tents looked very comfortable with the piles of rugs. It was such a hot night that Dinah fastened the tent-flaps right back, in order to get some air.

'That storm doesn't seem to have come,' she said, looking at the western sky to see if any big clouds were sweeping up. 'But it feels very thundery.'

'Here are the others,' said Lucy-Ann, as she saw Jack, Philip and Bill coming up from the shore. 'And Huffin and Puffin are still with them! Oh, Di – won't it be fun if we have two pet puffins!'

'I wouldn't mind *puffins*,' said Dinah. 'But I can't bear those rats. Hallo, Bill! Did you hear the aeroplane?'

'Good gracious, no! Was there one?' demanded Bill, with great interest. 'Where? How was it we didn't hear it?'

'We were making such a row,' said Jack, grinning. 'We shouldn't have heard a hundred aeroplanes.'

'It was funny,' said Lucy-Ann to Bill. 'I was watching the aeroplane when I saw something falling out of it. Something white.'

Bill stared, frowning intently. 'A parachute?' he said. 'Could you see?'

'No. It was too far away,' said Lucy-Ann. 'It might have been a parachute – or a puff of smoke – I don't know. But it did look as if something was falling slowly from the plane. Why do you look so serious, Bill?'

'Because – I've a feeling there's something – well, just a bit queer about these planes,' said Bill. 'I think I'll pop down to the motor-boat and send a message through on the wireless. Maybe it's nothing at all – but it just *might* be important!'

Chapter 12
Bill goes off on his own

Bill went off down the valley to the cove where the motor-boat was moored. His feet sank deeply into the soft earth. The children stared after him.

Lucy looked solemn – as solemn as Huffin and Puffin, who were leaning against Philip, standing upright, their big beaks looking heavy and clumsy.

'Oh dear – what does Bill mean? Surely we're not going to tumble into an adventure again! Up here, where there's nothing but the sea, the wind and the birds! What *could* happen, I wonder?'

'Well, Bill isn't likely to tell us much,' said Philip. 'So don't bother him with questions. I'm going to turn in. Brrrrr! It's getting a bit cold now. Me for that big pile of rugs! Huffin and Puffin, you'd better keep outside for the night. There'll be little enough room in this tent for you, as well as us three, Kiki and the rats.'

Huffin and Puffin looked at one another. Then, with one accord, they began to scrape the earth just outside the tent, sending the soil up behind them. Lucy-Ann giggled.

'They're going to make a burrow as near you as possible, Philip. Oh, aren't they funny?'

Kiki walked round to examine what the two puffins were doing. She got a shower of earth all over her and was very indignant.

'Arrrrrr!' she growled, and the two puffins agreed politely. 'Arrrrrrrr!'

Bill came back in about half an hour. All the children were cuddled up in their rugs, and Lucy-Ann was asleep. Dinah called out to him.

'Everything all right, Bill?'

'Yes. I got a message from London, to tell me that your mother is getting on as well as can be expected,' said Bill. 'But she's got measles pretty badly, apparently.

Good thing you're all off her hands!'

'What about your own message, Bill – about the aeroplane?' said Dinah, who was very curious over Bill's great interest in it. 'Did that get through?'

'Yes,' said Bill shortly. 'It did. It's nothing to worry your head about. Good night, Dinah.'

In two minutes' time everyone was asleep. Squeaker and his relations were only to be seen as bumps about Philip's person. Kiki was sitting on Jack's tummy, though he had already pushed her off several times. Huffin and Puffin were squatting in their new-made tunnel, their big coloured beaks touching. Everything was very peaceful as the moon slid across the sky, making a silvery path on the restless waters.

The morning dawned bright and beautiful, and it seemed as if the storm was not coming, for there was no longer any closeness in the air. Instead it was fresh and invigorating. The children ran down to the shore to bathe as soon as they got up. They ran so fast that Huffin and Puffin could not keep up, but had to fly. They went into the water with the children, and bobbed up and down, looking quite ridiculous.

Then they dived for fish, swimming with their wings under the water. They were very quick indeed, and soon came up with fish in their enormous beaks.

'What about giving us one for breakfast, Huffin?' called Philip, and tried to take a fish from the nearest puffin's beak. But it held on to it – and then swallowed it whole.

'You ought to teach them to catch fish for us,' said Jack, giggling. 'We could have grilled fish for breakfast then! Hey, get away, Puffin – that's my foot, not a fish!'

At breakfast they discussed their plans for the day. 'What shall we do? Let's explore the whole island, and give bits of it proper names. This glen, where we are now, is Sleepy Hollow, because it's where we sleep,' said Lucy-Ann.

'And the shore where we bathe is Splash Cove,' said Dinah. 'And where we first moored our motor-boat is Hidden Harbour.'

Bill had been rather silent at breakfast. Jack turned to him. 'Bill! What do *you* want to do? Will you come and explore the island with us?'

'Well,' said Bill, very surprisingly, 'if you don't mind, as you'll be very busy and happy on your own, I'll take the motor-boat and go cruising about a bit – round all these islands, you know.'

'What! Without *us*?' said Dinah in astonishment. 'We'll come with you, then, if you want to do that.'

'I'm going alone, this first time,' said Bill. 'Take you another time, old thing. But today I'll go alone.'

'Is there – is there anything up?' asked Jack, feeling that something wasn't quite right. 'Has something happened, Bill?'

'Not that I know of,' said Bill cheerfully. 'I just want to go off on my own a bit, that's all. And if I do a bit of exploring round on my own account, I shall know the best places to take you to, shan't I?'

'All right, Bill,' said Jack, still puzzled. 'You do what you want. It's your holiday too, even if it *is* a disappearing one!'

So Bill went off on his own that day, and the children heard the purr of the motor-boat as it went out to sea, and then set off apparently to explore all the islands round about.

'Bill's up to something,' said Philip. 'And I bet it's to do with those aeroplanes. I wish he'd tell us. But he never will talk.'

'I hope he comes back safely,' said Lucy-Ann anxiously. 'It would be awful to be stranded here on a bird-island, and nobody knowing where we were.'

'Gosh, so it would,' said Jack. 'I never thought of that. Cheer up, Lucy-Ann – Bill isn't likely to run into danger. He's got his head screwed on all right.'

The day passed happily. The children went to the cliffs and watched the great companies of sea-birds there. They sat down in the midst of the puffin colony and watched the queer, big-beaked birds going about their daily business.

Lucy-Ann wore a hanky tied round her nose. She couldn't bear the smell of the colony, but the others soon got used to the heavy sourness of the air, and anyway, the wind blew strongly.

Huffin and Puffin did not leave them. They walked or ran with the children. They flew round them, and they went to bathe with them. Kiki was half jealous, but having had one hard jab from Huffin's multi-coloured beak, she kept at a safe distance, and contented herself with making rude remarks.

'Blow your nose! How many times have I told you to wipe your feet? You bad boy! Huffin and puffin all the time. Pop goes huffin!'

The children sat in Sleepy Hollow after their tea and watched for Bill to come back. The sun began to set. Lucy-Ann looked pale and worried. Where was Bill?

'He'll be along soon, don't worry,' said Philip. 'We'll hear his boat presently.'

But the sun went right down into the sea, and still there was no Bill. The darkness closed down on the island, and there was no longer any point in sitting up and waiting. It was four anxious children who went into their tents and lay down to sleep. But none of them could sleep a wink.

In the end the girls went into the boys' tent and sat there, talking. Then suddenly they heard a welcome sound – *rr-rr-rr-rr-rr!* They all leapt up at once and rushed from the tent.

'That's Bill! It must be! Where's a torch? Come on down to the cove.'

They stumbled through the puffin colony, waking up many a furious bird. They got to the beach just as Bill came walking up. They flung themselves on him in delight.

'Bill! Dear Bill! What happened to you? We honestly thought you'd got lost!'

'Oh, Bill – we shan't let you go off alone again!'

'Sorry to have worried you so,' said Bill. 'But I didn't

want to return in the daylight in case I was spotted by an aeroplane. I had to wait till it was dark, though I knew you'd be worried. Still – here I am.'

'But, Bill – aren't you going to tell us anything?' cried Dinah. 'Why didn't you want to come back in daylight? Who would see you? And why would it matter?'

'Well,' said Bill slowly, 'there's something queer going on up here in these lonely waters. I don't know quite what. I'd like to find out. I didn't see a soul today, anywhere, though I nosed round umpteen islands. Not that I really expected to, because nobody would be fool enough to come up here for something secret, and let anything of it be seen. Still, I thought I might find some sign.'

'I suppose that bit of orange peel was a sign that some-one's here besides ourselves, on some other island?' said Lucy-Ann, remembering the piece that had bobbed against her fingers. 'But what are they doing? Surely they can't do much in this desolate stretch of waters – with nothing but islands of birds around.'

'That's what I'm puzzled about,' said Bill. 'Can't be smuggling, because the coasts of the mainland are very well patrolled at the moment, and nothing could get through. Then what is it?'

'Bill, you're sure nobody saw you?' asked Dinah anxious-ly. 'There might be hidden watchers on one of the islands, you know – and one might see you, without you seeing him.'

'That's true,' said Bill, 'but I had to risk that. It's not very likely, though. The risk of anyone coming to these islands and disturbing whatever secret game is going on, is very remote, and I don't think there would be sentinels posted anywhere.'

'Still – you *might* have been seen – or heard,' persisted Dinah. 'Oh, Bill – and you were supposed to be disappear-ing completely! Now perhaps your enemies have spotted you!'

'They would hardly be the same enemies that I've disappeared from,' said Bill with a laugh. 'I don't think anyone else would recognise me here, seen at a distance in a motor-boat. In any case they would just think I was a bird-man or a naturalist of some kind, who likes the solitude of these seas.'

They were soon back in their tents again, happy to have Bill with them in safety. The stars shone down from a clear sky. Huffin and Puffin shuffled down their burrow, glad that their new family had gone to rest. They did not approve of these night walks.

Lucy-Ann lay and worried. 'I can *feel* an adventure coming. It's on the way. Oh dear – and I did think this would be the very very last place for one.'

Lucy-Ann was quite right. An adventure *was* on the way – and had very nearly arrived.

Chapter 13
What happened in the night?

The next morning everything seemed all right. The children had forgotten their fears of the night before, and Bill joked and laughed as merrily as the others.

But all the same he was worried – and when an aeroplane appeared and flew two or three times over the islands, he made the children lie down flat, in the middle of the puffin colony, where they happened to be at that moment.

'I don't think our tents can be seen,' he said. 'I hope not, anyway.'

'Don't you want anyone to know we're here, Bill?' asked Jack.

'No,' said Bill shortly. 'Not at present, anyway. If you hear a plane, bob down. And we won't light a fire to boil a kettle. We'll have ginger-beer or lemonade instead.'

The day passed happily enough. It was very hot again and the children went to bathe half a dozen times, lying in the sun to dry afterwards. Kiki was jealous of Huffin and Puffin because they could go into the water with the children. She stood on the sandy beach, her toes sinking in, shouting loudly.

'Polly's got a cold, send for the doctor! A-tish-*ooooo!*'

'Isn't she an idiot?' said Jack, and splashed her. She was most annoyed and walked a bit farther back. 'Poor Kiki! What a pity! Poor pity, what a Kiki!'

'Yes, what a Kiki!' shouted Jack, and dived under the water to catch Bill's legs.

They took a good many photographs, and Huffin and Puffin posed beautifully, staring straight at the camera in a most solemn manner.

'I almost feel they'll suddenly put their arms round one another,' said Jack, as he clicked the camera. 'Thank you, Huffin and Puffin. Very nice indeed! But I wish you'd smile next time. Kiki, get out of the way – and leave that tent peg alone. You've already pulled up three.'

That night the sky was full of clouds and the sun could not be seen. 'Looks as if that storm might be coming soon,' said Bill. 'I wonder if our tents will be all right.'

'Well, there's nowhere else to go,' said Jack. 'Sleepy Hollow is about the most sheltered place on this island. And, as far as I've seen, there are no caves or anything of that sort.'

'Perhaps the storm will blow over,' said Philip. 'Phew, it's hot! I really think I must have one last bathe.'

'You've had eight already today,' said Dinah. 'I counted.'

Darkness came earlier that night, because of the clouds. The children got into their rugs, yawning.

'I think,' said Bill, looking at the luminous face of his wrist-watch. 'I think I'll slip along to the boat and send a message or two on my transmitter. I might get some news too, for myself. You go to sleep. I shan't be long.'

'Right,' said the boys, sleepily. Bill slipped out of the tent. The girls were already asleep and did not hear him go.

Philip fell asleep almost before Bill was out of the tent. Jack lay awake a few minutes longer, and pushed Kiki off his middle for the fifth time.

She went and stood on Philip's middle, and waited for a lump to come near her feet, which she knew would be one of the tame rats. When one did venture near, raising a little mound under the rug, Kiki gave a sharp jab at it. Philip awoke with a yell.

'You beast, Kiki! Jack, take her away! She's given me an awful peck in my middle. If I could see her I'd smack her on the beak.'

Kiki retired outside the tent till the boys were asleep again. She flew to the top of it, and perched there, wide awake.

Meanwhile Bill was in the cabin of the boat tuning in on the wireless. But because of the coming storm it was difficult to hear anything but atmospherics.

'Blow!' said Bill at last. 'I shan't get my messages through at this rate. I've a good mind to take the boat to the little channel – what is it the children call it? – Hidden Harbour. Maybe I could get the wireless going better there – it's so sheltered.'

It was very important to Bill to be able to use the wireless that night. He set the engine of the boat going, and was soon on his way to Hidden Harbour. He nosed in carefully and moored the boat.

Then he set to work on his wireless again. After a while he thought he heard some noise out to sea – a noise getting nearer and nearer. Bill turned off his wireless and listened, but the wind was getting up, and he heard nothing but that.

He turned the knobs again, listening intently for any message. He had got one through, and now he had been told to stand by and wait for an important announcement from headquarters.

The wireless fizzed and groaned and whistled. Bill waited patiently. Then, suddenly hearing a sound, he looked up, startled, half expecting to see one of the boys coming down into the cabin.

But it wasn't. It was a hard-faced man with a curious crooked nose who was staring down at him. As Bill turned and showed his face, the man uttered a cry of the utmost astonishment.

'*You!* What are *you* doing here? What do you know of . . .'

Bill leapt up – but at the same moment the man lunged out at him with a thick, fat, knobbly stick he held in his hand – and poor Bill went down like a ninepin. He struck his head against the edge of the wireless, and slid to the floor, his eyes closed.

The man with the crooked nose whistled loudly. Another man came to the small cabin and looked in.

'See that?' said the first man, pointing to Bill. 'Bit of a surprise, eh, to find *him* up here? Do you suppose he guessed anything?'

'Must have, if he's here,' said the second man, who had a short thick beard hiding a very cruel mouth. 'Tie him up. He'll be useful. We'll make him talk.'

Bill was tied up like a trussed chicken. He did not open his eyes. The men carried him out, and took him into a small boat, moored beside the *Lucky Star*. It was a rowing-boat. Into it went poor Bill, and the men undid their rope, ready to row back to their own motor-boat, which lay, perfectly silent, a little way beyond the island.

'Do you suppose there's anyone else with him?' asked the man with the crooked nose. 'There was no-one on board but him.'

'No. When his boat was sighted yesterday, we only saw one man aboard – and it was him all right,' said the man with the beard. 'If there'd been anyone else we'd have seen them. He's all alone. Ho! He didn't know he was being watched all the way back here last night.'

'I suppose there really *isn't* anyone else here,' said the

first man, who seemed very reluctant to go. 'Hadn't we better smash up the boat – just in case?'

'All right – and the wireless too,' said the man with the beard. He found a hammer and soon there were crashing sounds as the engine of the motor-boat was damaged and the beautiful little wireless was smashed to bits.

Then the men set off in their rowing boat with the unconscious Bill. They reached their motor-boat, and soon the purring of its engine getting fainter and fainter, sounded in the night. But nobody on Puffin Island heard it except Kiki and the sea-birds.

The children had no idea at all that Bill had not returned that night. They slept peacefully, hour after hour, dreaming of huffins and puffins, big waves and golden sands.

Jack awoke first. Kiki was nibbling at his ear. 'Blow you, Kiki!' said Jack, pushing the parrot away. 'Oh, goodness, here's Huffin and Puffin too!'

So they were. They waddled over to Philip and stood patiently by his sleeping face. 'Arrrrrr!' said Huffin lovingly.

Philip awoke. He saw Huffin and Puffin and grinned. He sat up and yawned. 'Hallo, Jack!' he said. 'Bill up already?'

'Looks like it,' said Jack. 'Probably gone to bathe. He might have waked us up though! Come on, let's wake the girls and go and bathe too.'

Soon all four were speeding to the sea, expecting to see Bill in the water. But he wasn't.

'Where is he, then?' said Lucy-Ann, puzzled. 'And good gracious – where's the boat?'

Yes – where was the boat? There was no sign of it, of course. The children stared at the cove, puzzled and dismayed.

'He must have taken it round to Hidden Harbour,' said Jack. 'Perhaps the wireless wouldn't work or something. It still feels stormy, and that might have upset it.'

'Well, let's go to Hidden Harbour then,' said Philip. 'Perhaps Bill got sleepy down there in the boat and thought he'd snuggle up in the cabin.'

'He's probably there,' said Dinah. 'Fast asleep too! Let's go and give him a shock. We'll halloo down into the cabin and make him jump. The sleepyhead!'

'Oh, I do hope he's there,' said Lucy-Ann, shivering as much with worry as with cold.

They dressed quickly, shivering a little, for the sun was hidden behind angry-looking clouds. 'I do hope the weather isn't going to break up, just as we've begun such a lovely holiday,' said Dinah. 'Oh, Huffin, I'm sorry – but you got right under my feet. Did I knock you over?'

The puffin didn't seem to mind having Dinah tread on it. It shook out its wings, said 'Arrrrr!' and hurried on after Puffin, who was trying to keep pace with Philip.

They went across the puffin colony, and came to the cleft in the cliffs. There, below them, lay the motor-boat, swaying very gently as waves ran up under her, and then ran back again.

'There she is!' said Dinah in delight. 'Bill *did* take her round to the harbour!'

'He's not on deck,' said Jack. 'He must be in the cabin. Come on.'

'Let's call him,' said Lucy-Ann suddenly. 'Do let's. I want to know if he's there.'

And before the others could stop her she shouted at the top of her voice. 'BILL! OH, BILL, ARE YOU THERE?'

No Bill came out from the cabin, and for the first time a little uneasiness crept into the children's minds.

'BILL!' yelled Jack, making everyone jump violently. 'BILL! Come on out!'

No sound from the boat. Suddenly panic stricken, all four children stumbled down the rocky ledge to the boat. They jumped on board and peered down into the little cabin.

'He's not there,' said Dinah, scared. 'Well, where is he, then?'

'He must be somewhere about, as the boat is still here,'

said Jack sensibly. 'He'll come along soon. Maybe he's exploring somewhere on the island.'

They were just turning away when Philip caught sight of something. He stopped and clutched Jack, turning very pale.

'What?' said Jack, frightened. 'What's up?'

Silently Philip pointed to the wireless. 'Smashed!' he said, in a whisper. 'Smashed to bits! Who did it?'

Lucy-Ann began to cry. Jack went up on deck and had a look round, feeling sick and upset. Then Philip gave an anguished howl from the cabin that sent the others running to his side.

'Look! The engine of the boat is smashed up too! Absolutely destroyed. My goodness – what's been happening here?'

'And where is Bill?' said Dinah, in a husky whisper.

'Gone. Kidnapped,' said Philip slowly. 'Someone came for him in the night. They don't know we're here, I suppose – they just thought Bill was alone. They've got him – and now we're prisoners on Puffin Island and we can't get away!'

Chapter 14
A few plans

Everyone felt suddenly sick. Lucy-Ann sat down in a heap. Dinah joined her. The boys stood staring at the smashed engine as if they couldn't believe their eyes.

'It must be a nightmare,' said Dinah at last. 'It can't be true. Why – why, everything was right as rain last night – and now . . .'

'Now the boat's smashed up so that we can't get away, the wireless is smashed so that we can't get a message through – and Bill's gone,' said Philip. 'And it isn't a dream. It's real.'

'Let's sit down in the cabin, all together,' said Lucy-Ann,

wiping her eyes. 'Let's sit close and talk. Let's not leave each other at all.'

'Poor Lucy-Ann!' said Philip, putting his arm round her, as she sat down unsteadily. 'Don't worry. We've been in worse fixes than this.'

'We haven't!' said Dinah. 'This is the worst fix we've *ever* been in!'

Kiki felt the tenseness of all the children. She sat quietly on Jack's shoulder, making little comforting noises. Huffin and Puffin sat solemnly on the deck, staring fixedly in front of them. Even they seemed to feel that something awful had happened.

In the cabin, sitting close together, the children felt a little better. Jack rummaged in a tiny cupboard beside him and brought out some bars of chocolate. The children had had no breakfast, and although the shock they had had seemed to have taken their appetites away, they thankfully took the chocolate to nibble.

'Let's try and think out carefully exactly what must have happened,' said Jack, giving a bit of his chocolate to Kiki.

'Well – we know that Bill was worried about something,' said Philip. 'Those planes, for instance. He felt certain something queer was going on up here. And that's why he went out by himself in the boat. He must have been seen.'

'Yes – and maybe in some way his enemies got to know he was here,' said Dinah. 'They could have followed him a long way back, using field-glasses to keep him in sight. Anyway – it's quite clear that they came looking for him here.'

'And found him,' said Jack. 'What a pity he went off to tinker with the wireless last night!'

'Well, if he hadn't, the enemy, whoever they are, would probably have searched the island and found us too,' said Dinah. 'As it is – they probably don't know we're here.'

'It wouldn't matter if they did know,' said Lucy-Ann, sniffing. 'They'd be quite sure we couldn't do any harm, living on an island we can't get off!'

'They got here – in a motor-boat probably,' went on Jack. 'Left the motor-boat out beyond, somewhere – and slipped inshore quietly in a rowing-boat. They must know this little channel – or maybe they saw a light from the boat. Bill would be sure to have the cabin light on, and it's a pretty bright one.'

'Yes. And they surprised him and knocked him out, I suppose,' said Philip gloomily. 'They've taken him away – goodness knows what'll happen to him!'

'They won't – they won't hurt him, will they?' said Lucy-Ann in rather a trembly voice. Nobody answered. Lucy-Ann began to cry again.

'Cheer up, Lucy-Ann,' said Philip. 'We've been in worse scrapes before, whatever Dinah says. We'll get out of this one all right.'

'How?' wept Lucy-Ann. 'I don't see *how* we can! You don't either.'

Philip didn't. He scratched his head and looked at Jack.

'Well – we've got to make *some* kind of plan,' said Jack. 'I mean – we must make up our minds what we are going to do to try and escape – and what we are going to do *till* we escape.'

'Won't Bill's friends come and look for us when they don't get Bill's messages through?' asked Dinah suddenly.

'Pooh! What would be the good of *that*?' said Philip at once. 'There are hundreds of these little bird-islands here. It might take years visiting and exploring every single one to find us!'

'We could light a fire on the cliff and keep it burning so that any searcher could see the smoke in the daytime and the flames at night,' said Dinah excitedly. 'You know – like ship-wrecked sailors do.'

'Yes, we could,' said Jack. 'Only – the enemy might see it too – and come along and find us before anyone else does.'

There was a silence. Nobody knew who the enemy were. They seemed mysterious and powerful and frightening.

'Well, I can't help it – I think we ought to follow Dinah's plan and light a fire,' said Philip at last. 'We've got to run the risk of the enemy seeing it and coming to find us. But we simply *must* do something to help anyone searching for us. We can keep a look-out for the enemy, and hide if they come.'

'*Hide! Where* can we hide?' asked Dinah scornfully. 'There isn't a single place on this island for *anyone* to hide!'

'No, that's true,' said Jack. 'No caves, no trees, except for those few little birches – and the cliffs too steep to explore. We really *are* in a fix!'

'Can't we do anything to help Bill?' asked Lucy-Ann dolefully. 'I keep on and on thinking of him.'

'So do I,' said Jack. 'But I don't see that we can do much to help ourselves, let alone Bill. Now – if we could escape from here – or wireless for help and get some of Bill's friends along – it would be *some*thing. But there doesn't seem anything at all to do except stay here and wait.'

'There's plenty of food, anyway,' said Dinah. 'Stacks of tinned stuff, and biscuits and potted meat, and Nestlé's milk and sardines . . .'

'I think we'd better strip the boat of them,' said Jack. 'I'm surprised the enemy didn't take what they could with them. Maybe they'll come back for them – so we'll take them first. We can hide them down some of the puffin burrows.'

'Let's have a bit of breakfast now,' said Philip, feeling better now that they had all talked the matter over and made a few plans. 'Open some tins and get some ginger-beer. Come on.'

They all felt better still when they had had something to eat and drink. They had put a cover over the poor smashed wireless. They couldn't bear to look at it.

Jack went up on deck when they had finished their meal. It was very close again, and even the wind seemed warm. The sun shone through a thin veiling of cloud, and had a reddish hue. 'That storm is still about,' said Jack. 'Come on, everyone. Let's get to work before it comes.'

It was decided that Philip and Dinah should hunt for driftwood to make a fire up on the cliff. 'We don't *know* that those aeroplanes we sometimes see belong to the enemy,' said Philip. 'If they don't, they may see our signal and come to circle round. Then they will send help. One might come today, even. So we'll get a fire alight. We'll bank it with dry seaweed. That will smoulder well and send up plenty of smoke.'

Jack and Lucy-Ann were to carry things from the boat to the tents in Sleepy Hollow. 'Take all the tins and food you can,' said Philip. 'If the enemy happened to come back at night and take it we'd be done. We should starve! As it is, we've got heaps to last us for weeks.'

The four children worked very hard indeed. Jack and Lucy carried sacks of tins from the boat to Sleepy Hollow. For the time being they bundled them in a heap by the tents. Kiki examined them with interest, and pecked at one or two.

'It's a good thing your beak isn't a tin-opener, Kiki,' said Jack, making the first little joke that day, to try and make Lucy-Ann smile. 'We shouldn't have much food left if it was.'

Philip and Dinah were also very busy. They took a sack each from the boat and wandered along the shore to pick up bits of wood. They found plenty at the tide-line and filled their sacks. Then they dragged them to the top of the cliff. Huffin and Puffin went with them, solemn as ever, sometimes walking, sometimes flying.

Philip emptied his sack of wood on a good spot. He began to build a fire. Dinah went off to fill her sack with dry seaweed. There was plenty.

Soon Jack and Lucy-Ann, emptying their own sacks in Sleepy Hollow, saw a spiral of smoke rising up from the cliff-top. 'Look!' said Jack. 'They've got it going already! Good work!'

The wind bent the smoke over towards the east. It was good thick smoke, and the children felt sure that it could be seen from quite a distance.

'One of us had always better be up here, feeding the fire, and keeping watch for enemies or friends,' said Philip.

'How shall we know which they are?' asked Dinah, throwing a stick on the fire.

'Well – I suppose we shan't know,' said Philip. 'What we'd better do if we see any boat coming is to hide – that is, if we can *find* anywhere to hide – and then try and discover if the searchers are enemies or friends. We are sure to hear them talking. We'd better get lots more wood, Di – this fire will simply *eat* it up!'

Lucy-Ann and Jack helped them when they had finished their own job. 'We've taken every single tin and every scrap of food out of the boat,' said Lucy-Ann. 'We really have got plenty to eat – and that rock-pool to drink from when we've finished the ginger-beer. There aren't an awful lot of bottles left now. Wouldn't you like to have dinner soon?'

'Yes. I'm jolly hungry,' said Philip. 'Let's have it up here, shall we? Or is it too much bother to fetch a meal here, Lucy-Ann? You see, one of us must keep the fire going all the time.'

'Well, it won't go out for a while, anyhow,' said Lucy-Ann. 'Bank it up with some more seaweed. Honestly, we feel fagged out, carrying all that stuff. Let's go to Sleepy Hollow and have a good rest and a jolly good meal.'

So they all returned to Sleepy Hollow, where the two tents flapped in the little breeze. They sat down and Lucy-Ann opened tins, and ladled the contents on to plates.

'You've got tinned salmon, biscuits and butter, tinned tomatoes and tinned pears,' she said.

Even Huffin and Puffin came closer than usual, to share such a nice meal. They would have eaten every scrap of the salmon if they could. Kiki preferred the tinned pears, but the children would only allow her one.

'Well, things would be a lot worse if we hadn't got all this nice food,' said Jack, leaning back in the warm sun, after a big meal. 'An adventure without good food would be awful! Kiki, take your head out of that tin. You've had more than any of us, you greedy glutton of a parrot!'

Chapter 15
A really terrible storm

The wind got up about five o'clock. It whipped the waves round the island until they towered into big white horses that raced up the beaches and broke with a sound of thunder. The sea-birds deserted the coves, and flew into the air, crying loudly. The wind took them and they soared for miles without beating a wing, enjoying themselves thoroughly.

Kiki didn't like so much wind. She could not glide or soar like the gulls and guillemots. It offended her dignity to be blown about too much. So she stayed close to the tents, which flapped like live things in the wind, and strained at the tent-pegs violently.

'Look here, we can't possibly watch the fire all night!' said Philip. 'We'll have to bank it up and hope for the best. Maybe it will send out a glow, anyway. Doesn't that sea-weed keep it in nicely? My goodness, the wind tears the smoke to rags now!'

The sun went down in a bank of angry purple clouds that gathered themselves together in the west. Jack and Philip stared at them.

'That's the storm coming up all right,' said Jack. 'Well, we've felt one coming for days – this hot weather was bound to end up like that. I hope the wind won't blow our tents away in the night.'

'So do I,' said Philip anxiously. 'Honestly, there's a perfect gale blowing up now! Look at those awful clouds! They look really wicked!'

The boys watched the clouds covering the sky, making the evening dark much sooner than usual. Philip put his hand into one of his pockets. 'My rats know there is a storm coming,' he said. 'They're all huddled up in a heap together right at the very bottom of my pocket. Funny how animals know things like that.'

'Jack!' called Lucy-Ann anxiously. 'Do you think the tents are safe? The wind is blowing them like anything!'

The boys went to examine them. They were as well pegged as they could be, but in this gale who knew what might happen?

'We just can't do anything about it but hope for the best,' said Jack rather gloomily. 'Philip, have you got your torch? We'd better be prepared to be disturbed in the night, if this gale goes on – we might have to re-peg one of the tents.'

Both boys had torches with new batteries, so that was all right. They put them down beside their beds when they cuddled up into their rugs that night. They all went early because for one thing it was getting very dark, for another thing it had begun to rain heavily, and for a third thing they were all very tired with the day's work. Kiki retired with the boys as usual, and Huffin and Puffin scuttled into their burrows nearby.

'Wonder what poor old Bill is doing,' said Jack to Philip, as they lay listening to the wind howling round them. 'I bet he's worried stiff about us.'

'It's a shame, just as we were all set for a glorious holiday,' said Philip. 'And now the weather's broken too! What on earth shall we do with ourselves if it goes on like this for days? It will be frightful.'

'Oh, it may clear up again when the storm is over,' said Jack. 'Golly, hark at the waves on the beaches round the island – and how they must be dashing against those steep cliffs! I bet the gannets and guillemots aren't getting much sleep tonight!'

'The wind's pretty deafening too,' said Philip. 'Blow it!

I feel so tired, and yet I can't possibly sleep with all this din going on. And gosh – what's that?'

'Thunder,' said Jack, sitting up. 'The storm is on us now all right. Let's go into the girls' tent, Philip. Lucy-Ann will be scared, if she's awake. A storm over this exposed little island won't be very funny.'

They crept into the other tent. The girls were wide awake and very glad to have them beside them. Dinah squeezed up into Lucy-Ann's rugs, and the boys got into Dinah's warm place. Jack flashed on his torch.

He saw that Lucy-Ann was very near tears. 'There's nothing to be frightened of, old thing,' he said gently. 'It's only a storm, and you're never frightened of those, Lucy-Ann, you know you aren't.'

'I know,' gulped Lucy-Ann. 'It's only that – well, the storm seems so wild and – and *spite*ful, somehow. It *tears* at our tent, and bellows at us. It seems alive.'

Jack laughed. The thunder came again and crashed more loudly than the waves on the shore. Kiki crept close to Jack.

'Pop, pop, pop!' she said, and put her head under her wing.

'Thunder doesn't pop, Kiki,' said Jack, trying to joke. But nobody smiled. The wind blew more wildly than ever and the children wished they had more rugs. It was very very draughty!

Then the lightning flashed. It made them all jump, for it was so vivid. For an instant the steep cliffs and the raging sea showed vividly. Then the picture was gone.

Crash! The thunder came again, this time sounding overhead. Then the lightning split the sky open again and once more the children saw the cliffs and the sea. They didn't seem quite real, somehow.

'Sort of unearthly,' said Philip. 'Gosh, hark at the rain! I'm getting spattered all over with it, though goodness knows how it's getting in here.'

'The wind's getting worse,' said Lucy-Ann fearfully.

'Our tents will blow away. They will, they will!'

'No, they won't,' said Jack stoutly, taking Lucy-Ann's cold hand in his. 'They can't. They . . .'

But at that very moment there came a rending sound, a great flap-flap-flap, something hit Jack across the face – and their tent was gone.

The four children were struck dumb for a moment. The wind howled round them, the rain soaked them. They had nothing over them to protect them – their tent had vanished. Vanished with the wild wind in the darkness of the night.

Lucy-Ann screamed and clutched Jack. He put his torch on quickly.

'Gosh – it's gone! The gale has taken it away. Come into our tent, quickly!'

But before the children could even get up from their rugs, the gale had taken the other tent too. It rushed by Philip, as he stood trying to help the girls up, and when he turned his torch to where his tent should be, there was nothing.

'Ours has gone too,' he cried, trying to out-shout the wind. 'Whatever are we to do?'

'We'd better get down to the boat – if we possibly can,' yelled Jack. 'Or do you think we shall be blown over? Had we better roll ourselves up in the ground-sheets and rugs and wait till the storm has blown itself out?'

'No. We'll be soaked. Better try for the boat,' said Philip. He dragged the girls up. Each of the children wrapped a rug round their shoulders to try and ward off the rain and the cold.

'Take hands and keep together!' yelled Philip. 'I'll go first.'

They took hands. Philip set off, staggering in the gale that was blowing in his face. Through the puffin colony he went, trying to keep on his feet.

Suddenly Dinah, who had hold of Philip's hand, felt him drag it away. Then she heard a cry. She called in fright.

'Philip! Philip! What's happened?'

There was no answer. Jack and Lucy-Ann came close to Dinah. 'What's up? Where's Philip?'

Jack's torch shone out in front of them. There was no Philip there. He had vanished completely. The children, their hearts beating painfully, stayed absolutely still in dismay and astonishment. Surely the gale hadn't blown him away!

'PHILIP! PHILIP!' yelled Jack. But only the wind answered him. Then all three yelled at the tops of their voices.

Jack thought he heard a faint answering cry. But where? It sounded at his feet! He swung his torch downwards, and to his immense surprise and fright he saw Philip's head – but only his head, on a level with the ground.

Dinah shrieked in fright. Jack knelt down, too dumbfounded to say a word. Just Philip's head – just Philip's . . .

Then he saw in a flash what had happened. Philip had trodden on soil so undermined by the puffins that it had given way – and he had fallen right through to a hole below. Jack could have cried with relief.

'Are you all right, Philip?' he yelled.

'Yes. Give me your torch. I've dropped mine. I've fallen through into a whopping big hole. There might be room for us all to shelter here for a bit,' shouted back Philip, the words being whipped away by the wind almost before Jack could hear them.

Jack gave Philip his torch. The boy's head disappeared. Then it came back again, looking very queer sticking up between some heather and a sea-pink cushion.

'Yes. It's an enormous hole. Can you all get down? We'd keep safe and dry here till the storm is over. Come on. It's a bit smelly, but otherwise not bad.'

Dinah slid through the opening of the hole and found herself beside Philip. Then came Lucy-Ann and then Jack. Jack had found Philip's torch and the two torches were now shone around the hole.

'I suppose the rabbits and the puffins together managed

to burrow so much that they have made an enormous hole,' said Jack. 'Look, there's a puffin burrow leading out of it over there – and one of the puffins staring in astonishment at us! Hallo, old son. Sorry to burst in on you like this.'

The relief of finding that Philip was safe, and of being out of the wild noise of the storm, made Jack feel quite light-headed. Lucy-Ann's sobs stopped, and they all looked round them with interest.

'*I* should think this was a natural cavity of some sort,' said Philip, 'with a layer of good soil, held together by roots and things, making a surface above – but all that burrowing by the puffins made it give way when I trod on it – and down I fell. Well, it's just what we wanted, for the moment.'

Above them, deadened by tangled heather and sea-pinks, the storm raged on. No rain came into the cavity. The thunder sounded very far away. The lightning could not be seen.

'I don't see why we shouldn't sleep here for the night,' said Jack, spreading out the rug he had taken from his shoulders. 'The soil is dry and soft – and the air must be good enough, because that puffin is still there, gazing at us. I say – I hope Huffin and Puffin are all right.'

They all spread out their rugs and lay down, cuddled up together. 'Congratulations on finding us such a fine home for tonight, Philip,' said Jack sleepily. 'Very clever of you indeed! Good night, everybody!'

Chapter 16
Next day

They all slept soundly in their queer shelter. They did not awake until late in the morning, because for one thing it was dark in the hole, and for another they had all been tired out.

Jack awoke first, feeling Kiki stirring against his neck. He could not think where he was. A little daylight filtered through the entrance of the hole, but not much. It was very warm.

'Arrrrrr!' said a guttural voice, and made Jack jump. 'Arrrrrr!'

It was the puffin which had come down its burrow to see them the night before. Jack switched on his torch and grinned at it.

'Good morning – if it is morning. Sorry to have disturbed you! I'll get Huffin and Puffin to explain to you, when we see them again.'

Philip woke and sat up. Then the girls stirred. Soon they were all wide awake, looking round the curious cavity, and remembering the events of the night before.

'What a night!' said Dinah, shuddering. 'Oh – when our tents blew away – I really did feel awful!'

'And when Philip disappeared, I felt worse,' said Lucy-Ann. 'What time is it, Jack?'

Jack looked at his watch and whistled. 'My word – it's almost ten o'clock. How we've slept! Come on, let's see if the storm is still going strong.'

He stood up and pulled away the overhanging heather that blocked up the narrow entrance to the hole. At once a shaft of blinding sunlight entered, and the children blinked. Jack put his head out of the hole in delight.

'Golly! It's a *perfect* day! The sky is blue again, and there's sunshine everywhere. Not a sign of the storm left. Come on, let's go up into the sunlight and have a look round.'

Up they went, giving each other a hand. Once they were out of the hole, and the heather fell back into place again, there was no sign of where they had spent the night.

'Wouldn't it make an absolutely marvellous hiding-place?' said Jack. The others looked at him, the same thought occurring to everyone at once.

'Yes. And if the enemy come – *that's* where we'll go,' said Dinah. 'Unless they actually walk over the place they can't possibly find it. Why – I don't know myself where it is now – though I've just come out of it!'

'Gosh, don't say we've lost it as soon as we've found it,' said Jack, and they looked about for the entrance. Jack found it in just the same way as Philip had the night before – by falling down it. He set an upright stick beside it, so that they would know the entrance easily next time. 'We might have to sleep down there each night now, as our tents have gone,' said Jack. 'It's a pity we've brought our rugs up. Still, they can do with a sunning. We'll spread them out on the heather.'

'Thank goodness that awful wind's gone,' said Dinah. 'There's hardly even a breeze today. It's going to be frightfully hot. We'll bathe.'

They had a dip in the quiet sea, which looked quite different from the boiling, raging sea of the day before. Now it was calm and blue, and ran up the sand in frilly little waves edged with white. After their bathe the children had an enormous breakfast in the spot where their tents had been.

Huffin and Puffin appeared as soon as the children arrived and greeted them joyfully.

'Arrrrrr! Arrrrrrr!'

'They're saying that they hope we've got a good breakfast for them,' said Dinah. 'Huffin and Puffin, I wish you'd eat rats. You'd be very useful then.'

Philip's rats had appeared again, now that the storm was over, much to Dinah's disgust. They seemed very lively, and one went into Jack's pockets to find a sunflower seed. It brought one out, sat on Jack's knee and began to nibble it. But Kiki pounced at once, and snatched the seed away, whilst Squeaker scurried back to Philip in a hurry.

'You're a dog in the manger, Kiki,' said Jack. 'You don't really want that sunflower seed yourself, and you won't let Squeaker have it either. Fie!'

'Fie fo fum,' said Kiki promptly, and went off into a screech of laughter, right in Jack's ear. He pushed her off his shoulder.

'I shall be deaf for the rest of the day! Lucy-Ann, look out for that potted meat. Huffin is much too interested in it.'

'Really – what with Kiki pinching fruit out of the tin, and Huffin and Puffin wanting the potted meat, and Philip's rats sniffing round, it's a wonder we've got anything ourselves!' said Lucy-Ann. But all the same, it was fun to have the creatures joining in and being one with them. Huffin and Puffin were especially comical that morning, for now that they were really friendly, they wanted to look into everything. Huffin suddenly took an interest in Dinah's fork and picked it up with his beak.

'Oh, don't swallow that, silly!' cried Dinah, and tried to get her fork away. But Huffin had a very strong beak, and he won the tug of war. He waddled away to examine the fork in peace.

'He won't swallow it, don't worry,' said Philip, tossing Dinah his own fork. 'It'll keep him quiet a bit if he plays with it for a while.'

The children's fire was, of course, completely out. It had to be pulled to pieces and lighted all over again. This was not so easy as before, because everything had been soaked during the night. Still, the sun was so very hot that it wouldn't be long before the wood and the seaweed were bone-dry again.

The children missed out dinner completely that day, because it had been twelve o'clock before they had cleared up their breakfast things. 'We'll have a kind of high tea about five,' said Jack. 'We've plenty to do – look for our tents – light the fire – find some more wood – and go and see if the motor-boat is all right.'

Their tents were nowhere to be seen. One or two pegs were found but that was all. 'The tents are probably lying on some island miles and miles away,' said Jack. 'Scaring the sea-birds there. Well – shall we sleep in that hole to-night?'

'Oh no, please don't let's,' begged Lucy-Ann. 'It's smelly. And it's so very hot again now that surely we could put our rugs on cushions of heather and sleep out in the open. I should like that.'

Philip looked up at the clear blue sky. Not a cloud was to be seen. 'Well,' he said, 'if it's like this tonight, it would be quite comfortable to sleep in the open. We'll plan to do that unless the weather changes. Let's find a nice cushiony place, and put our rugs there, and our other clothes, with the ground-sheets over them. Good thing the ground-sheets only blew up against those birch-trees and got stuck there!'

They found a nice heathery place, not too far from where Lucy-Ann kept the stores beneath the big ledge of stone, and piled their extra jerseys, their mackintoshes, their rugs and their ground-sheets there. Lucy-Ann had stored their spare clothes with the food under the ledge, but the rain had driven in, and had made them damp. So it was decided that it would be better to use them as extra bedclothes at night, and keep them under the ground-sheets during the daytime.

After they had done all this they went to see their fire, which was burning well now. They sat on the top of the cliff, with the birds crying all round them, and looked out on the calm, brilliantly blue sea.

'What's that?' said Lucy-Ann suddenly, pointing to something floating not far off.

'Looks like a heap of wood, or something,' said Philip. 'Wreckage of some sort. Hope it comes inshore. We can use it for our fire.'

It came slowly in with the tide. Philip put his glasses to his eyes. Then he lowered them again, looking so taken-aback that the others were scared.

'Do you know,' he said, 'that wreckage looks awfully like bits of the *Lucky Star*. And there's more bits over there, look – and I dare-say we should find some down on the rocks.'

There was a shocked silence. Nobody had even *thought* that the motor-boat might have been taken by the storm and battered. Jack swallowed hard. That *would* be a blow! He got up.

'Come on. We'd better go and see. Of course I suppose it was bound to be smashed up, but anyhow we couldn't have moved it. Gosh – what bad luck if the boat's gone! Even if the engine was smashed, it was still a boat. We might have rigged up a sail – or something . . .'

In silence the children left the fire on the cliff and made their way through the cleft, and down the rocky ledges to the little harbour.

There was no boat there. Only a bit of the mooring-rope was left, still tied round the rock nearby, its ragged ends fluttering in the tiny breeze.

'Look!' said Jack, pointing. 'She must have been battered up and down by great waves rushing in and out of the channel – see the paint on the rocks – and look at the bits of wood about. When the rope broke she must have been taken right out of the channel, and then beaten to bits against the cliffs. What a frightful shame!'

The girls had tears in their eyes, and Philip had to turn away too. Such a lovely boat! Now she was nothing but masses of wreckage which they could burn on their fire. Poor *Lucky Star*. *Unlucky Star* should have been her name.

'Well, nothing we could have done would have helped,' said Jack at last. 'The storm would have wrecked her anyway – though if Bill had been here, and the boat was all right, he would have taken her round to Splash Cove and we could have dragged her right up the beach, out of reach of the waves. It wasn't our fault.'

They all felt sad and downcast as they left the little harbour and went back. The sun was going down now, and the evening was very peaceful and beautiful. There was hardly any wind at all.

'I can hear an aeroplane again!' said Lucy-Ann, her sharp ears picking up the distant throbbing before the others. 'Hark!'

Far away a small speck showed low down in the blue sky. The boys clapped their glasses to their eyes. Jack gave an exclamation.

'It's dropping something, look! Philip, what is it? Is it a parachute?'

'It looks like a small parachute – with something underneath it, swinging to and fro,' said Philip, his eyes glued to his glasses. 'Is it a man? No, it doesn't look like a man. Then what in the world is it? And why is the plane dropping things here? Gosh, I wish Bill was here to see this. There *is* something queer going on. Something the enemy are doing. I shouldn't be surprised if they get the wind up when they see our smoke and come along to search the island. Tomorrow one of us must always be on the lookout, from the cliff.'

Puzzled and anxious, the children went back to Sleepy Hollow. It was time for high tea, and Lucy-Ann and Dinah prepared it in silence. They were in the middle of an adventure again – and they couldn't possibly get out of it.

Chapter 17
A boat, a boat!

'Do you think it's worth while keeping the fire going, if the aeroplanes belong to the enemy?' asked Lucy-Ann at last.

'Well, if we're *ever* to be rescued, we shall have to show some kind of signal,' said Jack. 'We'll have to risk the aeroplanes seeing it. Perhaps, when no messages come through from Bill, motor-boats will come looking for us. Then they will see our signal, and come to the island.'

'I hope they do,' said Dinah. 'I don't want to be here for months. And it would be awful in the winter.'

'Good gracious! Don't talk about being here for the *winter!*' said Lucy-Ann, in alarm. 'Why, it's only May!'

'Dinah's looking on the black side of things as usual,' said Philip.

Dinah flared up. 'I'm not! I'm being sensible. You always call being sensible "looking on the black side of things." '

'Oh, don't quarrel just now, when we all ought to stick by each other,' begged Lucy-Ann. 'And *don't* put those rats near Dinah, Philip – don't be mean just now!'

Philip snapped his fingers and the rats scurried back to his pockets. Kiki snorted.

'Three blind mice, see how they run, pop goes Kiki!'

'Arrrrr!' said Huffin, agreeing politely. It was really very comical the way he and Puffin seemed to talk to Kiki. They never said anything but 'Arrrr,' but they said it in many different tones, and sounded quite conversational at times.

That night the children slept out in the open. It was a beautiful calm night, and the stars hung in the sky, big and bright. Lucy-Ann tried to keep awake to watch for shooting stars, which she loved, but she didn't see any.

Her bed was very comfortable. The children had chosen thick heather to put their groundsheets and rugs on, and had used their extra clothes for pillows. A tiny breeze blew against their cheeks and hair. It was lovely lying there with the stars shining peacefully above, and the sound of the sea in the distance.

'It's like the wind in the trees,' thought Lucy-Ann sleepily. 'And the wind in trees is like the sound of the sea. Oh dear, I'm getting muddled – muddled – mud—'

The weather was still lovely the next day, and the spiral of smoke from the signal fire went almost straight up in the air, there was so little wind. Jack and Philip took a good many bird-photographs, and Jack looked longingly over the steep bird-cliff, wishing he could climb down a little way and take some photographs of the birds there.

'Bill said not,' said Philip. 'And I think we oughtn't to. Suppose anything happened to us boys, what would the girls do? We've got heaps of fine photographs without bothering to take the eggs and birds on those ledges.'

'I wish the puffins had laid eggs,' said Jack. 'I haven't found a single puffin egg yet. It's a bit too early, I suppose. How sweet baby puffins must look! I wish I could see some.'

'Well, you're likely to, as things have turned out,' said Philip, with a half-comical groan. 'We may be here for quite a long time.'

It was arranged that one or other of the children should always be on the look-out somewhere on the bird-cliff. From there it was possible to see nearly all round the island, and no enemy could approach without being seen when still far off. That would give plenty of time for the others to be warned, and for all of them to go into hiding.

'We'd really better hide all the tins and things that are under our ledge, down in that hole, hadn't we?' said Lucy-Ann, when the plans were made. 'They might easily be found.'

'We'll stuff heather round them,' said Jack. 'It would be an awful bore to have to keep going down into the hole to fetch all the food each time we wanted something to eat.'

So clumps of heather were most realistically tucked under the rocky ledge where Lucy-Ann kept the tins. Nobody would guess it wasn't growing, it looked so natural there.

'We'd have plenty of time to chuck our clothes and things down into the hidey-hole, if we saw anyone coming,' said Jack. 'I'll take first watch. I shan't be a bit bored, because there are so many birds up there – and Kiki is such a clown with them, it's as good as a pantomine to watch her.'

Two days went by without anything exciting happening at all. Once they heard another aeroplane, but didn't see it. More wreckage was thrown up on the beach from the unfortunate *Lucky Star*. The children bathed and ate and slept, and took it in turns to keep watch, but they saw nothing to worry them at all.

Kiki always kept watch with Jack. Huffin and Puffin kept watch with Philip. Once another puffin came too near Philip for Huffin's liking, and the bird ran at it with his head down, growling *arrrrrrr* like an infuriated dog. Their big beaks locked together, and Philip almost cried with laughter as he watched the curious battle.

'The battle of beaks,' he called it, when he described it to the others afterwards. 'Talk about stags locking their antlers together and fighting – those two puffins were every bit as fierce with their huge beaks.'

'Who won?' asked Lucy-Ann, with great interest. 'Huffin, I suppose?'

'Of course,' said Philip. 'He not only won, he chased the other one right into its burrow, and they both came out again at another entrance, with Huffin winning the race. I'm surprised the other poor bird had any feathers left by the time Huffin had finished with him.'

On the afternoon of the third day, Jack was sitting up on the top of the bird-cliff. It was his turn to look out. He gazed lazily out to sea. There was just a little more breeze that day, and the waves had frills of white as they came in to shore.

Jack was thinking about Bill. Where was he? What had happened to him? Had he been able to escape, and if so, would he come quickly to rescue the four children? And what was Aunt Allie thinking? Had she heard that there was no word from Bill, and was she worried?

Jack thought deeply about all these things, listening to the different cries of the sea-birds about him, and watching their graceful flight over the sea. Then his eyes suddenly picked out something far off on the water.

He stiffened like a dog that suddenly sees something unusual. He reached down for his field-glasses and put them to his eyes. He had soon got the something out there into focus – and he saw that it was a small motor-boat.

'Enemies,' he thought, and was about to leap to his feet when he remembered that whoever was in the boat might also have glasses, and might see him. So he wriggled away on his tummy, and not until he was well down into the little valley did he jump up and run to the others.

'Hi!' he called breathlessly, as he tore down to Sleepy Hollow, where the others were having a laze. 'There's a boat coming!'

They all sat up at once. Lucy-Ann's green eyes were wide with excitement and fright. 'Where? How far away?'

'Quite a way off. It will take them about ten minutes to come in and tie up. We'd better chuck everything down into the hole at once.'

'What about the fire?' said Dinah, grabbing her pile of jerseys and coats.

'Have to leave that. They've already seen the smoke

anyway,' said Jack. 'Come on, quick! Get a move on, Lucy-Ann!'

It didn't take long to part the heather over the narrow entrance to the hole and hurl everything down. Jack removed the stick he had put there to mark the place.

'No good leaving a signpost for them,' he said, trying to make Lucy-Ann smile. She gave him a watery grin.

'No – everything cleared up?' said Philip, looking round. He pulled at the clumps of heather they had been lying on, which had got rather flattened, but the springy plants were already getting back into position themselves. Philip picked up a spoon that someone had left lying there and popped it into his pocket. There really did seem to be nothing left now that would show that the children had been there a few minutes before.

'Come on, Tufty! Don't wait about!' said Jack, in a fever of impatience to get below ground. The girls were already safely in the hole. Jack slid down himself and Philip followed almost at once.

Jack pulled the heather neatly over the hole. 'There! Now unless anybody actually treads in the hole, as Philip did the other night, we're safe. Nobody would ever know there was a big cavity underground.'

'I feel like a puffin,' said Philip. 'I feel I'd like to burrow. What about digging a nice little burrow for each of us to lie in?'

'Oh, don't make jokes now,' begged Lucy-Ann. 'I don't feel like jokes. I feel – I feel all sort of tight and breathless. And my heart simply *couldn't* beat any louder. Can you hear it?'

Nobody could. But then, their own hearts were beating so fast and so loudly that it was no wonder they could not hear anybody else's.

'Can we whisper?' asked Dinah, in a loud whisper that made everyone jump.

'I should think so. But don't talk out loud,' said Jack.

'And if we hear anyone coming, listen with all your might, so that we shall know if it's friends or enemies. It would be *too* awful if it was friends and we let them go away without finding us.'

That was indeed an awful thought – almost worse than the thought of being found by an enemy. Everyone sat quietly, holding their breaths, listening with all their might. 'Friend or enemy, friend or enemy, friend or enemy,' said a voice in Lucy-Ann's mind, and she couldn't stop it saying the words over and over again. 'Friend or . . .'

'Sh,' came Jack's whisper, suddenly. 'I can hear something.'

But it was only Huffin and Puffin arriving in the hole. They pushed the heather aside and flopped in, giving the children a terrible shock. The heather swung back, and the puffins stared in the darkness, trying to find Philip.

'You wretched birds!' scolded Philip. 'You might have shown them our hiding-place. Don't you dare to say a word!'

'Arrrrrr!' said Huffin deeply. Philip gave him an angry push, and the bird walked away in astonishment. It was the first time he had ever had an angry word or gesture from his beloved Philip. He hopped up to the beginning of a nearby burrow, followed by Puffin, and began to walk up it, very much offended. The children were glad to hear them go.

'Sh!' came Jack's whisper again, and the others clutched one another. 'They're really coming now! Shhhhhhhh!'

Chapter 18
The enemy – and Kiki

The thud of footsteps could be felt in the dark hole below ground. Then came the sound of voices. 'We'll search the whole place. *Somebody* must be keeping that fire going!'

'There's nowhere much to hide on this small island,' said

another voice. 'Nobody could get down those sheer cliffs, so that rules them out. And there's obviously nobody in this valley – except these ridiculous birds.'

There came the sound of a match being struck. One of the men was evidently lighting a cigarette. He tossed the match away – and it came trickling through the heather into the hole where the trembling children crouched. It fell on to Dinah's knee and she almost squealed.

'They're dreadfully near,' everyone was thinking. 'Dreadfully, dreadfully near!'

'Look here,' said one of the men's voices, suddenly. 'What's this? A bit of chocolate wrapping-paper! I bet the hiding-place isn't far off.'

The children's hearts almost stopped beating. Philip remembered that a bit of his chocolate-paper had blown away on the wind and he hadn't bothered to go and pick it up. Blow! Blow! Blow!

Jack felt about for Kiki. Where was she? She had slid off his shoulder, but he couldn't feel her anywhere near. He did hope she wouldn't suddenly make one of her loud remarks, just under the very feet of the men.

Kiki had gone up the burrow, after Huffin and Puffin. The two puffins were now staring at the men who had come to hunt. They stood at the entrance of a burrow, looking fixedly with their crimson-circled eyes.

'Look at those silly chaps,' said one man. 'Whatever are these ridiculous birds, with beaks like fireworks about to go off?'

'Don't know. Puffins or sea parrots, or something,' said the other man.

'Huffin and Puffin,' said Kiki, in a loud, conversational sort of voice. The men jumped violently and looked all round. Kiki was in the burrow behind Huffin and Puffin and could not be seen. She didn't want to push past them in case they nipped her.

'Did you hear that?' said the first man.

'Well – I thought I heard something,' said the other. 'But these birds all round make such a racket.'

'Yes – a frightful din,' said the first man.

'Din-din-dinner,' announced Kiki and went off into one of her cackles of laughter. The men stared in alarm at the two solemn puffins. 'I say – surely those birds can't *talk*?' said one. Kiki went on laughing and then coughed deeply.

'It's a bit queer, isn't it?' said the first man, rubbing his chin and staring at Huffin and Puffin. It seemed as if it really must be the two puffins who were talking and coughing. Kiki could not be seen.

Huffin opened his beak. 'Arrrrrr!' he said solemnly.

'There!' said the man. 'I saw him that time. They *are* talking birds. Sea parrots perhaps – and parrots talk, don't they?'

'Yes, but they have to be taught,' said the other. 'And who taught these two?'

'Oh, come on – don't let's waste any time on the ridiculous creatures,' said the first man, turning to go. 'We'll go down to the shore and walk along it to make sure there's no one there. Pity the boat's been smashed up in the gale. We could have taken off some of the food in it.'

Kiki gave an imitation of a motor-bike in the distance, and the men stopped suddenly in astonishment.

'I could have sworn that was a motor-bike!' said one, with a half-ashamed laugh. 'Come on – we're hearing things. Wait till I get hold of whoever is on this island – making us waste time hunting like this!'

To the children's enormous relief the men's voices got fainter and fainter and at last could not be heard at all. Kiki came back into the cave.

'What a pity, what a pity!' she said in a whisper, cracking her beak.

'Kiki, you awful idiot, you nearly gave the game away!' whispered Jack. 'Get on my shoulder – and I warn you, if you say just one more word, I'll tie your beak up with my hanky.'

'Arrrrrrrr!' said Kiki, and settled down with her head under her wing. She was offended.

For what seemed like hours the children sat silently in the hole underground. They heard no more voices, and no more footsteps shook the ground nearby.

'How long have we got to stay here like this?' whispered Dinah at last. She was always the first to get impatient. 'I'm cramped.'

'I don't know,' said Jack, in a whisper that seemed to fill the underground cavity. 'It would be dangerous to pop my head out and take a look-see.'

'I'm hungry,' said Lucy-Ann. 'I wish we'd brought something to eat down with us. And I'm thirsty too.'

Jack wondered whether or not to risk sticking his head out. Just as he was making up his mind that he would, everyone in the hole heard a far-off, very welcome noise.

'It's the engine of their motor-boat being started up,' said Jack in relief. 'They must have given up the hunt, thank goodness. We'll give them a few minutes, then I'll hop out.'

They waited for five minutes. The motor-boat's engine sounded for a little while, then grew fainter and finally could not be heard at all.

Jack cautiously put his head out. He could see and hear nothing but puffins. Huffin and Puffin were squatting nearby and got up politely when they saw his head.

'Arrrrrrr!' they said.

Jack got right out of the hole. He lay down flat, put his field-glasses to his eyes and swept the sea around. At last he spotted what he was looking for – the motor-boat going away at top speed, getting smaller and smaller in the distance.

'It's all right!' he called down to the others. 'They're almost out of sight. Come on out.'

Soon they were all sitting in Sleepy Hollow, with the girls getting a meal ready, for by this time they were once again ravenous. The ginger-beer had now all been drunk, so they drank the water from the rock-pool, which was rather warm from the sun, but tasted very sweet. The rain from the storm had swelled it considerably.

'Well, that was a jolly narrow escape,' said Philip, his spirits rising as he tucked into slices of 'Spam.' 'I really did think one of them would tumble in on top of us.'

'Well, what do you suppose *I* felt like when the match

one of them used fell through the hole and bounced on my knee?' said Dinah. 'I nearly let out a yell.'

'Kiki almost gave the game away too,' said Jack, putting potted meat on a biscuit. 'Calling out "din-din-dinner" like that. I'm ashamed of you, Kiki.'

'She's sulking,' said Dinah, laughing. 'Look at her – standing with her back to you, pretending not to take any notice. That's because you were cross with her.'

Jack grinned. He called to Huffin and Puffin, who were, as usual, standing patiently beside Philip. 'Hey, Huff and Puff – come and have a tit-bit. Nice birds, good birds, dear Huff and Puff.'

Huffin and Puffin walked over to Jack, doing their sailor-roll from side to side. They solemnly took a bit of biscuit from Jack's fingers. But that was more than Kiki could stand. She whisked round and screeched at the top of her voice.

'Naughty boy, naughty boy, naughty boy! Poor Polly, poor Polly! Polly's got a cold, put the kettle on, naughty boy, naughty boy!'

She rushed at the startled puffins and gave them a sharp jab with her curved beak. Huffin retaliated at once, and Kiki stepped back. She began to screech like a railway-train, and the two puffins hurriedly returned to Philip's knees, where they stood and stared in alarm at Kiki, ready to dart down a burrow at a moment's notice.

The children roared with laughter at this little panto-mime. Kiki went to Jack, sidling along in a comical manner. 'Poor Kiki, poor Kiki, naughty boy, naughty boy!'

Jack gave her a tit-bit and she sat on his shoulder to eat it, looking triumphantly at Huffin and Puffin. 'Arrrrrr!' she said to them, sounding like a snarling dog. 'Arrrrrr!'

'All right, Kiki. Don't *arrrrr* any more just by my ear,' said Jack. 'And I should advise you not to go too near Huffin for a bit. He won't forget that jab of yours.'

'Do you think it'll be safe to sleep out of doors again

tonight?' asked Dinah, clearing up the meal. 'I don't fancy sleeping down that hole again, somehow.'

'Oh, I should think it would be all right,' said Jack. 'I don't somehow think those fellows, whoever they were, will come along in the dark of night. Pity we didn't catch a glimpse of them.'

'I didn't like their voices,' said Lucy-Ann. 'They sounded hard and horrid.'

'What a good thing that storm blew our tents away the other night!' said Dinah suddenly. 'If it hadn't, we wouldn't have stumbled on that hole, and been able to use it as a hiding-place. We wouldn't have known *where* to go, but for that.'

'That's true,' said Philip. 'I wonder if those men will come back again. We'll go on keeping watch anyway, and keep the fire going. It's our only hope of rescue – and Bill's only hope too, I should think – because if nobody comes to rescue us, certainly nobody will rescue Bill!'

'Poor Bill!' said Lucy-Ann. 'He wanted to disappear – and he has.'

'Those men must have put our fire out,' said Jack, suddenly noticing that there was no smoke. 'The wretches! I suppose they thought they'd put it out, and then, if it was lighted again, and the smoke rose up, they'd know for certain that somebody was here.'

'We'll jolly well go and light it again,' said Philip at once. 'We'll show them we're going to have our fire going if we want to. I guess they don't want it going, in case somebody does happen to come along and see it. They won't want people exploring this part of the world at the moment.'

So they all went up to the cliff-top, and set to work to light the fire again. The men had kicked it out, and the ashes and half-burnt sticks were scattered everywhere.

It didn't take long to get it going again. The children built it up carefully, and then Philip lighted it. It caught at once and flames sprang up. When it was going well, the children banked it with seaweed, and at once a thick spiral of smoke ascended in the air.

'Ha! You men! I hope you have caught sight of our signal again!' cried Jack, facing out to sea. 'You can't beat us! We'll get the better of you yet, you'll see!'

Chapter 19
Someone else comes to the island

The children were now very brown with the sun. 'If Mother could see us now, she wouldn't call us "peaky," ' said Philip. 'And you've got back all your freckles, Jack and Lucy-Ann, and a few hundreds more!'

'Oh dear!' said Lucy-Ann, rubbing her brown freckled face. 'What a pity! I did think I looked so nice when my freckles faded away during measles.'

'I seem to be losing count of the days,' said Jack. 'I can't for the life of me make out whether today is Tuesday or Wednesday.'

'It's Friday,' said Philip promptly. 'I was counting up only this morning. We've been here quite a time now.'

'Well – is it a week since we left home?' wondered Dinah. 'It seems about six months. I wonder how Mother is getting on.'

'She must be feeling a bit worried about us,' said Philip. 'Except that she knows we're with Bill and she'll think we're quite all right, even if she doesn't get messages.'

'And we're not with Bill and we're not all right,' said Lucy-Ann. 'I wish I knew where Bill was and what was happening to him. If only we had a boat, we could go off in it and try to find where he was. He must have been taken to the west of us somewhere – because that's where the planes seem to be.'

'Well – we're not likely to get a boat,' said Philip. 'Come

on – let's go up on the cliff-top and see to the fire. The smoke doesn't seem very thick this morning. Huffin and Puffin, are you coming?'

'Arrrrrrr!' said both Huffin and Puffin, and walked along beside Philip. Huffin had taken to bringing fish as a little present for Philip, and this amused the children immensely. The first time that Huffin had waddled up with the fish in his big beak, the children hadn't been able to make out what he was carrying. But when he came nearer they roared with laughter.

'Philip! He's got six or seven fish in his beak for you – and do look how he's arranged them!' cried Jack. 'Heads and tails alternately in a row all down his beak! Huffin, how did you do it?'

'Thanks awfully, old chap,' said Philip, as Huffin deposited the fish beside the boy. 'Very generous of you.'

Now Huffin brought fish two or three times a day, much to the children's amusement. Philip knew how to prepare it for cooking over the fire, and the children ate the bigger fish with biscuits and tinned butter. Huffin solemnly accepted a piece cooked, and seemed to enjoy it just as much as raw. But Puffin would not touch it.

'Well, as long as we've got Huffin to provide us with fish, we shan't starve,' said Jack. 'Kiki, don't be so jealous. If Huffin wants to be generous, let him.'

Kiki tried to head off Huffin when he arrived with fish. She could not catch fish herself, and did not like the way Huffin brought presents to the little company.

'Naughty, naughty, naughty boy!' she screeched, but Huffin took no notice at all.

The children were sitting by the fire, idly throwing sticks on it, and stirring it now and again to make it flare up a little. A spiral of smoke rose up, bent northwards. Jack took up his field-glasses and swept the lonely sea with them. You never know when friends – or enemies – might turn up.

'Hallo! There's a boat again!' cried Jack suddenly, his

glasses focused on something small far away. 'Philip, get your glasses.'

The boys gazed through them, whilst the girls waited impatiently. They could see nothing with their bare eyes – not even a speck on the sea.

'Is it the same boat as before?' said Philip. 'It's getting nearer – we shall soon be able to find out.'

'It looks a different one to me,' said Jack. 'Smaller. And it's coming from a different direction. That might just be a trick though – to make us think it was a friend.'

'How shall we know?' said Lucy-Ann. 'Have we got to go and hide again?'

Jack gave his glasses to her to look through. He turned to Philip, a gleam in his eye. 'Philip – there's only *one* man this time – he'll have to leave his boat moored somewhere, if he's come to look for us. What about capturing it?'

'Golly! If only we could!' said Philip, his face glowing. 'It's a motor-boat – a small one – but big enough to take us all easily.'

'Capture it! But how?' demanded Dinah, her eyes glued on the approaching boat. 'The man would see us easily, come running up, and capture *us*!'

'Here, let me have my glasses back,' said Philip, tugging them away from Dinah. 'That's the worst of you, Di – you will always make your turn so long!'

'Now let's think a bit,' said Jack, his eyes bright. 'That fellow can't be coming to *rescue* us, because anyone knowing we were all alone here would send a bigger boat, and probably more men, in case they had to tackle our enemy. If Bill had managed to get word to anyone, that's what they would do. Therefore, it seems to me that this boat is not one sent to rescue . . .'

'So it's probably a trick of the enemy's,' continued Philip. 'They may or may not know there are only children here – it depends on how much Bill has told them – but they might quite easily send someone who would pretend *not* to be an

119

enemy, so as to take us in – and then we would be persuaded to get into his boat to go to safety – and he'd take us off somewhere to join Bill as prisoners.'

'Oh!' said Lucy-Ann, who didn't like the sound of this at all. 'Well, I certainly shan't get into his boat. Jack, what are we going to do?'

'Now listen,' said Jack. 'I really have got a good idea – but it needs all of us to carry it out, you girls too.'

'Well, what have we got to do?' said Dinah impatiently.

'We'll find out where he's going to moor his boat,' said Jack. 'He'll either go into that little channel where the *Lucky Star* was – or pull her up on a sandy beach. We shall soon know, because we shall watch.'

'Yes, what then?' asked Lucy-Ann, beginning to feel excited.

'Well, Dinah and I will hide nearby,' said Jack. 'The man will walk up on to the island, to look for us – and you and Lucy-Ann, Philip, must go and meet him.'

'Oh, I *couldn't*', said Lucy-Ann, in alarm.

'All right then – you stay put somewhere,' said Jack, 'and Philip can meet him. And Philip, somehow or other you've got to get this fellow into that underground hole. We can easily keep him prisoner there – and if we can block him in somehow, with plenty of food, we can take the boat and go.'

There was a silence whilst everyone digested this remarkable plan. 'But how am I to get him into the hole?' asked Philip at last. 'It sounds a bit like " 'Won't you come into my parlour?' said the spider to the fly" – and somehow I don't think that the fly will oblige this time!'

'Can't you just take him through the puffin colony, and walk him near the hole – and then trip him up?' asked Jack impatiently. 'I'm sure *I* could do it all right.'

'Well, you do it then,' said Philip, 'and I'll hide near the boat to capture it. But suppose you don't trip the man up and make him fall into the hole and be a prisoner? What about the boat? What shall I do with it?'

'Well, silly, you'll hop into it, if you find that I haven't been able to manage the man, and you'll get out to sea,' said Jack. 'And there you'll stay till it begins to get dark, when you can creep in and see if you can find us and take us off. But you needn't worry – I shall get that fellow all right. I shall tackle him just like I tackle chaps at rugger, at school.'

Lucy-Ann gazed at Jack in admiration. What it was to be a boy!

'Well, I'll help too,' she said. 'I'll go and meet him with you.'

'We shall have to pretend to believe all he says,' said Jack. 'Every word! It'll be funny – him trying to take *us* in with a cock-and-bull story, and us doing the same!'

'I hope he won't be very fierce,' said Lucy-Ann.

'He'll pretend to be quite harmless, I expect,' said Jack. 'Probably say he's a naturalist, or something – and look very simple and friendly. Well – so shall I!'

'The boat's getting quite near,' said Philip. 'There *is* only one man. He's wearing dark glasses because of the sun.'

'To hide his fierce eyes, I expect,' said Lucy-Ann fearfully. 'Not because of the sun. Do we show ourselves?'

'Only two of us,' said Jack. 'You and I will get up, Lucy-Ann, and wave like mad, standing beside the fire. And mind, whatever story I tell, you've got to back me up. Philip, you and Dinah mustn't show yourselves.'

'Where's he going to park his boat?' wondered Dinah. 'Oh, he's making straight for the channel! He knows it then!'

'There you are, you see!' said Jack. 'Nobody would make straight for that hidden channel unless he had been here before. He's quite probably one of the men who came in that bigger boat.'

This did seem very likely indeed, for the boatman made straight for the little channel as if he had been there before. Just as he came near the cliffs Jack and Lucy-Ann stood up and waved. The man waved back.

'Now, Dinah – you and Philip get down among the rocks that lead to the little harbour,' said Jack. 'There are some big ones there you can crouch behind till he's moored his boat, and comes up to find us here. Then down you must go and hop into the boat ready to go out to sea if we fail in *our* part. If we *don't* fail, things will be fine – we shall have a prisoner we can hold as hostage – and a boat to escape in!'

'Hurray!' said Philip, feeling suddenly excited.

'Hip-hip-hip!' said Kiki, flying down to Jack's shoulder. She had been on an expedition of her own somewhere – probably chivvying the gulls around, Jack thought.

'You can join in the fun, Kiki,' said Jack. 'And mind you say all the right things!'

'Send for the doctor,' answered Kiki, solemnly. 'Pop goes the doctor!'

'He's going into the channel,' said Philip. 'Come on, Dinah – time we hid! Good luck, Jack and Lucy-Ann!'

Chapter 20
Mr Horace Tipperlong gets a shock

The man guided the motor-boat expertly into the narrow channel of water, where the *Lucky Star* had been battered to pieces. He saw the bit of broken rope still round one of the rocks, and looked at it, puzzled.

Dinah and Philip were crouching behind two or three large rocks further up the cliff. They could not see what the man was doing, for they were afraid of being spotted if they peeped out.

Jack and Lucy-Ann were waiting on the cliff-top. Lucy-Ann was nervous. 'My knees feel funny,' she complained to Jack. He laughed.

'Don't be a baby. Buck up, knees! Now – here he comes. You needn't say a word if you don't want to.'

The man came up the rocky steps that led to the top of the cleft in the cliff. He was a thin fellow, rather weedy, with skinny legs. He wore shorts and a pullover. He had been burnt by the sun, and his skin was blistered.

He had a thin little moustache, and a high forehead on which the hair grew far back. He wore very dark glasses indeed, so that it was quite impossible to see his eyes. He did not look anybody to be very much feared, Jack thought.

'Hallo, hallo, hallo,' said the man, as he and the children

met. 'I was astonished to know there were people on this island.'

'Who told you?' asked Jack at once.

'Oh, nobody,' said the man. 'I saw your spire of smoke. Whatever are you doing here? Is there a camp of you, or something?'

'There might be,' said Jack, airily. 'Why have you come here?'

'I'm an ornithologist,' said the man, very earnestly. 'You won't know what that means, of course.'

Jack grinned to himself. Considering that he and Philip thought themselves very fine ornithologists, this amused him. But he wasn't going to let this man know that.

'Orni—orni—ornibologist?' he said innocently. 'What's that?'

'Well, my lad, it's a student of bird life,' said the man. 'A bird-lover, one who wants to know all he can about birds and their ways.'

'Is that why you've come here, then – to study birds?' asked Lucy-Ann, thinking she ought to say something. Her knees had stopped shaking and feeling funny, now that she saw the man was not at all fearsome.

'Yes. I've been to this island before, years and years ago, when I was a lad,' said the man. 'And I wanted to come again, though I had a job finding it. I *was* surprised to see your smoke going up. What's it for? Playing at shipwrecked sailors, or something? I know what children are.'

It was plain that the man knew very little about children, and thought the two to be much younger than they were. 'He'll be reciting "Humpty Dumpty" to us in a moment,' thought Jack, with a secret grin.

'Do you know a lot about birds?' said Jack, not answering the man's question.

'Well, I don't know a *great* deal about sea-birds,' said the man. 'That's why I've come to these islands again. I know more about ordinary birds.'

'Aha!' thought Jack, 'he says that because he is afraid I'll ask him a few questions about the birds here.'

'We've got two tame puffins,' said Lucy-Ann suddenly. 'Would you like to see them?'

'Oh, very much, my dear, very much,' said the man, beaming at her. 'By the way, my name is Tipperlong – Horace Tipperlong.'

'Tripalong?' said Lucy-Ann, with a giggle, thinking it was a very good name for this man, who walked with curious mincing steps. Jack wanted to laugh.

'No, no – Tipperlong,' said Horace, and smiled all over his face at Lucy-Ann. 'What is your name?'

'My name's Lucy-Ann,' she said. 'And my brother's name is Jack. Are you coming to see the puffins? It's this way.'

'I should also like to meet whoever is in charge of you,' said Mr. Horace Tipperlong. 'And – er – where is your boat?'

'It was smashed up in a storm,' said Jack solemnly. Mr. Tipperlong tut-tutted with sympathy.

'How dreadful! Then how were you going to get back home?'

'Look out,' said Jack, just saving Horace as he was about to plunge down a puffin's burrow. 'This place is undermined by the puffins. Mind where you go!'

'My word – what a lot of birds!' said Horace Tipperlong, standing still. He had been so engrossed in polite talk that he did not seem to have noticed the amazing colony of puffins. Another black mark against him! Jack could not believe that a real ornithologist would walk half-way through the puffins without exclaiming at them.

'Extraordinary! Most astonishing! I don't remember ever seeing so many birds together before,' said Horace. 'And all those thousands on the cliffs too. Well, well, well! And do you mean to say you really have got two tame puffins? I can hardly believe it.'

'They're Philip's,' said Lucy-Ann, and she could have bitten out her tongue.

'I thought you said your brother's name was Jack,' said Horace enquiringly.

'She must have made a mistake,' said Jack, saying the first thing he could think of. They were getting very near the entrance of the underground hole now. Look out, Mr. Horace Tipperlong!

Lucy-Ann began to feel nervous. Suppose this man Trip-along, or whatever his name was, didn't fall into the hole when Jack tripped him – suppose instead he went for Jack? Suppose – well, suppose he had a revolver? He didn't *look* a desperate sort of a man, but you never knew. Lucy-Ann looked at the pockets of his shorts to see if she could spy anything like a lump in the shape of a revolver there.

But his pockets were so bulged out with dozens of things that it was impossible to tell. Jack nudged her. 'Keep out of the way now,' he said in a very low voice. Lucy-Ann obediently slipped behind, her heart beating fast.

Jack came to the entrance of the hole. A stick marked it as usual, for it really was almost impossible to find without some sort of signpost. Horace tripped along, looking short-sightedly through his dark glasses – and then, to his enormous astonishment, Jack put out a leg, pushed him, and tripped him right over. He fell at the side of the hole – but before he could get up, Jack had given him a shove – and right into the hole he went, crash!

Jack had a stout stick in his hand, which he had picked from the pile beside the bonfire. He parted the heather and looked into the hole. In the dim light he could see Horace Tipperlong sitting up, and he heard him groaning.

Tipperlong looked up and saw Jack. 'You wicked boy!' he said angrily. 'What do you mean by this?'

His glasses had fallen off in his headlong dive. His eyes certainly did not look very fierce. They looked rather weak and watery. He held his head as if he had hurt it.

'Sorry,' said Jack, 'but it had to be done. Either you caught us – or we caught you. We needn't go on pretending any more. We know quite well what gang you belong to.'

'What are you talking about?' cried the man, and he stood up. His head popped out of the hole. Jack raised his stick at once.

'Get back!' he said fiercely. 'You're our prisoner. You took Bill, didn't you? – well, now we've taken *you*. If you attempt to clamber out, I shall hit you on the head with this. You just try it.'

Horace hastily retreated. Lucy-Ann looked white and scared. 'Oh, Jack – is he hurt? Jack, you won't really hit him, will you?'

'I jolly well will,' said Jack. 'Think of Bill, Lucy-Ann – and our poor *Lucky Star* – and us stranded here because of this fellow and his precious friends. Don't you realise that if he gets out and back to his boat, they'll send heaps more, and won't rest till they've got us? Don't be feeble!'

'Well – I don't want to see you hit him,' said Lucy-Ann. 'Dinah wouldn't mind a bit, but I'm not strong-minded like Dinah.'

'Look here – will you kindly tell me what all this nonsense is about?' shouted Horace. 'I never heard of such a thing! Here I come to a bird-island, which, as far as I know, certainly isn't a crime – and you two kids lead me here, trip me up, and shove me down this hole. I've hurt my head badly. And now you say if I try to get out, you'll brain me. You nasty little creatures!'

'I'm really very sorry about it,' said Jack again, 'but there wasn't anything else to be done. You realise that with our boat gone – and Bill disappeared – we had to get a boat somehow. We can't stay here for the rest of our lives.'

Horace was so amazed and upset at this speech that he stood up again. He sat down hurriedly when he saw Jack's stick. 'But look here – do you really mean to say you're now going to take my boat? I never heard such brazen cheek.

You wait till I get hold of the people in charge of you, my boy – you'll get the worst hiding you've ever had in your life.'

Chapter 21
Horace does not like Puffin Island

'Lucy-Ann – see if you can spot either Philip or Dinah,' ordered Jack. 'Philip will probably be in the boat, ready to start her up, if he has to – but Dinah will possibly be looking out to see if there is any sign from us.'

Lucy-Ann stood up. She saw Dinah standing a good way off, waiting anxiously at the top of the cleft in the cliff. Philip was not to be seen. Presumably he was down in the boat.

Lucy-Ann waved violently. 'It's all right. We've got him in the hole!' she yelled.

Dinah waved back, then disappeared. She had gone to tell Philip. Soon the two appeared again, and came through the puffin colony at top speed to hear what had happened.

'We got him,' said Jack proudly. 'Easy as pie. Down he went, plonk!'

'Who's there?' enquired Horace plaintively. 'Is that somebody else? Look here – you've just *got* to tell me what's going on here. I'm all at sea.'

'That's where we'll be soon, I hope,' grinned Jack. 'And in your boat! Philip, meet Mr. Horace Tripalong.'

'Gosh – is that really his name?' said Philip.

The incensed Mr. Tipperlong roared up the hole. 'My name is TIPPERLONG and I'll thank you to remember it. Ill-mannered children! You wait till I make a complaint about you, and get you punished. I never heard of such behaviour in all my life.'

'You can't blame him for being wild,' said Jack. 'He says

he's a—a—I say, Mr. Tripalong, what did you say you were?'

'An ornithologist, ignorant boy!' yelled Mr. Tipperlong.

'Golly, what's that?' said Philip innocently, and the others giggled.

'You let me out of this,' commanded Mr. Tipperlong, and his head appeared cautiously near the entrance of the hole, ready to bob back if necessary.

It *was* necessary. 'Look here,' said Jack, exasperated, 'do you want me to give a you a good old conk on the head before you know I mean what I say? Because I will! I don't *want* to; but I will! I bet you gave old Bill a few blows before you captured him. What's sauce for the goose is sauce for the gander.'

'You're talking double-Dutch,' said Horace, in a disgusted voice. 'I think you must be mad. Do you mean to tell me you kids are all alone on this island? I don't believe a word you say. You tell whoever is in charge of you to come and have a word with me. If you think I'm going to stay here much longer, you're mistaken. I've never met such unpleasant children in my life. I suppose you're all playing at being Just Williams. *Pah!*'

This was a lovely noise. Kiki, who had been listening with surprise and enjoyment to the animated conversation, now joined in.

'Pah! Pooh! Pah! Pop!'

She flew to the edge of the hole and looked in. 'Pah!' she said again, and went off into a cackle of laughter.

Horace looked up in fresh alarm. Was that really a parrot at the hole entrance – saying 'pah' and 'pooh' to him in that rude way?

'Is that – is that one of the tame puffins you told me about?' he asked doubtfully.

'I thought you were an ornithologist,' said Jack in scorn. 'Kiki is a parrot. I should have thought anyone would have known that!'

'But – how can a parrot live here?' said Horace. 'It's not a sea-bird. Oh, this is all a dream. But what a very silly dream!'

At that moment a puffin came down the end of the burrow that led into the back of the hole.

'Arrrrrr!' it announced in a deep and guttural voice. Mr. Tipperlong jumped violently. All he could see in the dimness of the hole was a baleful eye and a big and many-coloured beak.

'Go away,' he said weakly. 'Shoo!'

'Shoo!' said Kiki from the hole entrance in great delight. 'Pah! Pooh! Shoo! Arrrrrrrr!'

'You're all mad,' said poor Horace. 'I'm mad too, I suppose. Shoo, I tell you!'

The puffin said *arrr* again and then went back up its burrow. Judging by the flow of *arrrs* that came down the hole, it was telling its wife all about the peculiar puffin-man it had just seen in the hole.

'What are we going to do now we've got him?' said Philip in a low voice. 'I suppose he *is* an enemy? I mean, – he does sound rather a goof, doesn't he?'

'All part of a clever plan,' said Jack. 'He's no ornithologist. He's been told to dress up like a goofy one and act the part. Some bird-men *are* awful goofs, you know. We've met them. Well, this one is just about too goofy for words – he's over-acting, if you know what I mean. I'm glad he hasn't got a revolver. I've been afraid of that all the time.'

'Yes. So was I,' admitted Philip. 'There may be one in the boat. I hope there is. It might come in useful. Well, what are we going to do?'

'Do you think he can hear what we're saying?' said Lucy-Ann, looking frightened.

'No, not if we talk as low as this,' said Philip. 'Jack, the boat is a nice little bit of work. Smaller than the *Lucky Star*, but it has a little cabin and will easily take us all, and some food.'

'Are there oars in it, in case we want to cut out the engine and go in quietly to shore anywhere?' asked Jack.

'Yes,' said Philip. 'I noticed those. Have you got a good plan, Jack? I keep on and on thinking, but all I can make up my mind about is to sail off in the boat – but where to I don't know. We want to escape – but we want to escape *to* somewhere. And not out of the frying-pan into the fire, either. We'd better do it soon, too, because if dear old Tripalong doesn't get back to the gang with news pretty soon they'll send others here.'

'Yes, I'd thought of all that too,' said Jack, and the girls nodded. 'The thing is – shall we try to make for the outer islands and find one where a few fishermen live, and try to get help? Or shall we try for the mainland? Or shall we hunt for Bill?'

There was a silence. Everyone was thinking hard. Lucy-Ann spoke first.

'I vote for hunting for Bill,' she said. 'We could try that first, anyway – and then make for safety afterwards if we're not successful. But I do think we ought to try to find Bill first.'

'Good for you, Lucy-Ann,' said Jack. 'That's what *I* think. Now for some more planning.'

Horace Tipperlong suddenly demanded their attention again. 'Stop all that talk, talk, talk,' he cried fretfully. 'I'm ravenous – and thirsty too. If you're going to try and starve me to death, say so. But at least let me know.'

'We're not going to starve you. Don't be an ass,' said Jack. 'Lucy-Ann, open some tins and give them to him. And chuck him down some biscuits too. Dinah, fill a pan with water from the pool.'

'Right, chief,' grinned Dinah, and went off to the pool in the rocks. Horace was handed down the full pan of water, and some tins and biscuits. He began to eat hungrily. The sight of the food made the others feel hungry too.

'We'll have a feed as well,' said Philip. 'Shall I take a turn at holding the stick and sitting by the hole, Jack?'

'Yes,' said Jack. 'But mind – give him a good old conk if he so much as shows a hair!'

This was said in a very loud voice, so that Horace was sure to hear. But Horace said nothing. Apparently he was willing to bide his time now.

The children were soon devouring a tinned chicken, tinned peas which they ate without heating, and a tinned fruit salad with tinned cream, washed down with water from the pool.

'Jolly good,' said Jack, with a comfortable sigh. 'I feel better. Wonderful what food does to you!'

'It would make me sick if I ate as much as you've just eaten,' said Dinah. 'You're a greedy pig. You ate twice as much as anyone else.'

'Can't help it,' said Jack. 'I was twice as hungry. Now then – lower your voices, please – we'll make our plans.'

'Shall we set out at night?' said Philip in a low voice.

'No,' said Jack at once. 'We'd never see our way, even in the moonlight. We'd better set off first thing tomorrow morning, about dawn. We'll hope old Tripalong is asleep then, so that we can get a good start without his interrupting us.'

'Yes – because we'll have to leave the hole unguarded when we all go to the boat,' said Lucy-Ann.

'I'd thought of that,' said Jack. 'You three can go to the boat, take food with you, and our clothes and rugs – get everything absolutely ready – and then, when you're ready to start, give me a yell and I'll come tearing along to join you. You can send Dinah up to the top of the cleft to wave.'

'And by the time Horace has realised nobody is on guard to conk him on the head, we'll be out to sea in his boat!' said Dinah, enjoying the thought. 'Poor old Horace! I feel quite sorry for him.'

'I don't,' said Jack unfeelingly. 'If he's Bill's enemy, he's jolly well mine. He deserves all he's got – honestly, except for being tripped into the hole, he's got nothing much to complain about. I shan't block him in, when we leave, and put food there, as I thought we would at first. It won't matter if he gets out once we're gone. And I shouldn't think it will be long before some others of the gang come along to see why he hasn't turned up at home – wherever that is!'

'It seems a bit of a wild-goose chase to try and find Bill, with all these scores of islands to choose from,' said Philip. 'But I shouldn't feel comfortable if we didn't have a shot, anyway.'

'Nor should I,' said Jack. 'Bill's often come to *our* rescue, in other adventures. It's time we went to his – if only we can find him. I suppose there's no doubt but that the enemy have taken him to their headquarters on some island or other here.'

'Don't you think it would be a good idea if we got everything ready this evening?' said Dinah suddenly. 'You know – all the food in the boat – and rugs and clothes and things – so as not to have to waste a single minute getting ready tomorrow morning. You said you wanted to set off at dawn.'

'Yes – that's a good idea,' said Jack. 'I'll take a turn at the hole with the stick now if you like, Philip – and you help the girls to carry things down to the boat. What a bit of luck capturing one like that! I must say I think we've been pretty clever.'

'Pah!' said Kiki. 'Pooh! Pah!'

'Sorry you don't agree, old thing,' said Jack. 'Very sorry. But I still think we *have* been very clever!'

'We'd better leave some food for Tripalong, hadn't we?' asked Dinah. 'I mean – I know the gang will be along in a day or two to see what has happened to him – but he'll have to have things to eat till they come.'

'Yes. Leave him some tins and a tin-opener,' said Jack. 'And, Philip, were there any rugs in the boat, belonging to him?'

'Yes,' said Philip. 'I'll bring them back here, after I've

taken some food to the boat. We'll chuck them down to him. I think we're being awfully kind to our enemy.'

Horace didn't think so. He got all upset again after a bit, and began to shout wildly down in the hole.

'This has gone on long enough. You let me out, you little villains! Wait till I get my hands on you! What is the meaning of this, I'd like to know?'

'Oh, don't keep up the pretence any more, Mr. Horace Tripalong,' said Jack, bored. 'We're enemies, both of us, and you know it. You open up a bit and tell me where Bill is and a few things more. You might get off more lightly in the end, if you do.'

'Who's this Bill you keep talking about?' said Horace in an exasperated tone. 'Look here, are you playing at pirates or Red Indians or what? I never heard of anyone being kept prisoner down a hole like this, by a pack of villainous children!'

'No – I never heard of it either, now I come to think of it,' said Jack. 'Well, dear Horace, if you won't admit what we all know, keep quiet.'

'Pah!' said Horace, aggravated beyond words.

'Pah!' said Kiki at once, and went to the hole entrance. She looked down.

'Pah! Naughty boy! Pop goes the weasel! How many times have I told you to shut the door? God save the King! Pah!'

Mr. Tipperlong listened in amazed horror. Was he really and truly mad? *Could* that be a parrot talking to him so rudely?

'I'll wring that bird's neck,' he said fiercely, and got up.

'Ring the bell, please!' said Kiki, and went off into one of her cackles. Then she poked her head in again and screeched like a railway engine in a tunnel. It was absolutely deafening in the hole below, and Horace fell back on the ground defeated.

'Mad! Quite mad! All mad!' he muttered, and, putting his head in his hands, he said no more.

Chapter 22
The enemy

The three children, accompanied by Huffin and Puffin, made various journeys to and from Sleepy Hollow with food, rugs and clothes. Philip brought back a pile of rugs from the boat and thrust them down the hole entrance. They descended on poor Horace and enveloped him. He was very much startled, but glad to find in a moment or two that his captors were actually offering him something warm and soft to lie on.

He arranged them underneath himself. Ah, that was more comfortable. He began to think longingly of all the things he would do to those children, once he got free.

At last everything was in the motor-boat, ready for the early start. It was now getting dusk. Philip, Lucy-Ann and Dinah came and sat beside Jack.

'I suppose one or other of us must keep watch over the hole all night, in case Horace escapes?' whispered Philip. Jack nodded.

'Yes. We can't risk his getting out, just as we've got everything set. You take first watch, Philip. We won't let the girls watch, because I'm pretty sure they wouldn't hit Horace good and hard if he popped his head out.'

'I would!' said Dinah indignantly. 'Lucy-Ann is the softie, I'm not.'

Lucy-Ann said nothing. She felt sure she wouldn't be able to hit Horace hard. Anyway the boys decided that only they should keep watch, so that was all right.

The sun had gone down into the sea. The sky was pricked with the first few stars. The children lay about comfortably on the heather, talking in low voices. There was no sound from Horace. Perhaps he was asleep.

Philip's three rats, which had suddenly begun to look very grown-up, came out to sniff the evening air. Dinah removed herself at once. Huffin and Puffin regarded the rats with fixed eyes. Kiki yawned and then sneezed. Then she coughed in a very hollow manner.

'Shut up, Kiki,' said Jack. 'If you want to practise your awful noises, go up on the cliff and make the seagulls and guillemots listen.'

'Arrrr!' said Huffin solemnly.

'Huffin agrees with me,' said Jack.

'Pah!' said Kiki.

'And pah to you,' said Jack. 'Now shut up, Kiki, do. It's a lovely evening. Don't spoil it with your pahing and poohing.'

Just as he finished speaking, there came a noise from far out to sea – a very small noise at first, hardly heard above the sound of the sea and the wind – but becoming quite unmistakable after a while.

'A motor-boat!' said Jack, sitting upright. 'Now what in the world . . .'

'Have they come to look for Horace already?' said Philip, in a low voice. 'Blow! This upsets our plans like anything!'

Nothing could be seen on the darkening sea, but the noise came nearer and nearer. Jack clutched Philip and spoke in his ear.

'There's only one thing to do. We must all go and get into our boat now, this very minute – and get out to sea. We mustn't let the enemy see the boat in the channel there, or they'll take it, and our only chance will be gone. Come on, quickly!'

Silently the four children rose to their feet. Kiki flew to Jack's shoulder, not uttering a sound. Huffin and Puffin, who had retired to their burrow, came out again. They flew beside the hurrying children, not even remarking *arrrr* to one another.

Across the puffin colony they went, stumbling and staggering between the hundreds of burrows. Up the little slope of the cliff and over to the cleft in the rock. Down the rocky ledges, be careful, be careful! And into the rocking boat, their breath coming fast and their hearts beating like hammers.

'Start her up,' ordered Philip, and Jack started the engine. Philip threw off the mooring-rope and it skittered into the boat by the girls' feet. In a moment more they were backing gently out of the little channel.

Soon they were right out of it. Philip went to the east a little. It was almost dark now.

'We'll stop the engine,' said Philip. 'And wait here till the other boat goes into the channel, because I expect she'll make for it. I don't want to bump into her. And the men on board her might hear our engine.'

So the engine was stopped, and the motor-boat swung up and down gently as waves ran beneath her to the rocky cliffs some way off.

The sound of the other boat's engine was now very loud. Philip wished he had gone a bit further off after all. But the bigger boat swung by without stopping and then nosed its way into the hidden harbour. The children, crouching in their boat, straining their eyes, had just been able to make out a dark shape and that was all.

The other boat's engine stopped and peace came back into the night. Some of the sea-birds, disturbed, uttered a few wild cries and then flew back to their roosting-places on the ledges.

'Horace will be glad to be rescued,' said Dinah at last.

'Yes, he'll probably be out of the hole already,' said Jack. 'He'd soon know when we were gone. I've no doubt there'll be a lot of bad language going on when they find out how we imprisoned poor Horace – and gosh, when they find out we've taken his boat . . .'

'Arrrrrr!' said a deep voice from the rail round the deck.

The children jumped in the darkness. 'Oh – it must be Huffin or Puffin,' said Philip, pleased. 'Fancy them coming with us. I do think that's friendly of them.'

'They're sweet,' said Lucy-Ann, and put out her hand to

Huffin. Both the puffins were there, sitting side by side in the darkness. Kiki flew to join them.

'What are we going to do now?' said Dinah. 'Dare we go off in the dark? We might bump into rocks and wreck the boat.'

'We'll have to stay here till the first light of day,' said Philip. 'Then we'll set off, and hope the men on the island won't hear our engine, and come after us!'

'We shall have got a good start,' said Jack. 'Well, what about having a snooze, if we're going to stay here? Where's the anchor? Shall we let it down? I don't fancy drifting about at the mercy of the waves all night long.'

Whilst the boys were busy, the girls laid out rugs, mackintoshes and jerseys to lie on. It was a lovely warm night, and nobody minded.

'It's so nice to have the stars above us instead of a ceiling or a tent roof,' said Lucy-Ann, snuggling down. 'I don't feel a bit sleepy, somehow. I suppose it's all the excitement. I've got used to this adventure now. Oh dear, how glad I am that I didn't have to hit Horace on the head! I should have dreamt about that for ages.'

They lay for some time, talking. They all felt very wide awake indeed. Huffin and Puffin appeared to be awake too, because they occasionally remarked *arrr* to one another. Kiki was on Jack's feet.

She also was wide awake, and began to recite the nursery rhymes she knew: 'Humpty dumpty, puddingy pie, ding dong bell, ring his neck!'

'Shut up!' said Jack. 'We're trying to go to sleep, you tiresome bird!'

'I hope Huffin and Puffin stay with us,' said Lucy-Ann. 'Wouldn't it be lovely if we could take them home with us?'

'Shut up!' said Kiki, and cackled.

'Parrots are not allowed to say that,' said Jack severely, and sat up to tap her on her beak. But she had promptly put her head under her wing, so he couldn't.

'Artful creature,' said Jack, and heard a faint 'Pah!' from under Kiki's wing.

Just as Lucy-Ann was falling off to sleep, the others sat up so suddenly that she was jerked awake. 'What's the matter?' she began. And then she knew.

The engine of the other motor-boat was going again. Lucy-Ann sat up with the others, her eyes straining through the darkness.

'They must have found Horace, heard his report, and all have gone back on board,' said Jack. 'They are evidently not going to spend the night here. Look – here they come – gosh, they've got their lights on this time.'

'Jack—Jack! They'll be going back to their headquarters,' said Philip urgently. 'Let's follow them. Get the anchor up, quick. They won't hear our engine because theirs makes such a row. Come on, let's follow them! They'll take us to where Bill is!'

The men's motor-boat had swung round when it had come from the channel, and was now headed out to sea. It was not long before the children's boat set off in its wake. They could not hear the other boat's engine because of their own, and they knew that theirs would not be heard by the men for the same reason.

Huffin and Puffin were still on the deck-rail. Clearly they meant to go wherever the children went. Lucy-Ann thought it was nice to have such staunch, loyal friends, even if they were only puffins. Kiki was on Jack's shoulder again, her beak to the breeze.

'All aboard,' she kept saying. 'All aboard. Pah!'

The first boat sped along quickly. It was easy to follow because of its light. The children stood with their noses to the wind in silence. Lucy-Ann spoke first.

'This adventure is getting more adventurous,' she said. 'Oh dear – it really is!'

Chapter 23
The secret lagoon

For a long time the two boats sped across the sea. 'It's the Sea of Adventure!' Lucy-Ann thought. 'Anything might happen here. Oh, I do hope we find Bill. Things always seem right when he's with us.'

'You girls had better have a nap,' said Jack at last. 'You'll be tired out. Philip and I will keep awake and take turns at the wheel. You snuggle down and go to sleep.'

So they did, and it wasn't long before both girls were asleep and dreaming of swings and hammocks, because of the swinging, swaying motion of the boat they were in.

After a good long time, Jack spoke to Philip. 'Tufty – do you see the light flashing over there? It must be a signal of some sort, I should think. The boat in front is heading towards it. I hope we're soon coming to our journey's end, because the moon will be up soon, and we might be seen.'

'That light must be a guide to the boat – or perhaps to an aeroplane,' said Philip. 'Blow, here comes the moon! – out of that bank of clouds. Well, she's not very bright, that's one good thing.'

By the light of the moon the boys could see an island looming up in front of the boats. To the left was another island, two or three miles away from the first, or so it seemed to the boys.

'Look here, Jack – we don't want to drive right into the jaws of danger,' said Philip, 'which is what we shall do if we follow the first boat right up to that island it's heading for. I think it would be better to go to that other one, yonder, look – we could probably see enough in the moonlight to make out a cove to land in. We could pull this boat into safety between us.'

'Right,' said Jack, swinging the wheel round. Now they were no longer following the first boat. It was soon out of sight, and was probably by now safely in some little harbour. Their own boat headed for the further island. By the time they got there their eyes were used to the moonlight, and they could see everything fairly clearly.

'Doesn't seem very rocky,' said Jack, nosing in gently. 'No – all sand and fine shingle. I'll run her straight up this beach, Philip. Be ready to jump out as soon as she stops.'

The girls awoke and scrambled out of their wraps. Jack ran the boat straight up the shingly beach. It drove into the fine shingle and stopped. Philip sprang out.

'Can't shift her at all,' he panted, when he and the others had tried to pull the boat further up. 'Let's chuck out the anchor and let her be. It's nearly low tide now, so we'll just paddle out and drop the anchor, and give the boat a push – it will be quite all right then, if the sea keeps calm.'

The boys did this and then lay on the shingle to get their breath. They were both very tired. They almost fell asleep as they lay there.

'Come on, boys,' said Dinah, at last. 'Bring some rugs and find a sheltered place somewhere. You're half asleep.'

'Well, we're safe till the morning anyway,' said Jack, as he stumbled up the beach with the others, almost asleep as he walked. 'Nobody knows we're here. Another bird-island, I suppose.'

They came to a low cliff. Lucy-Ann saw a dark cave at the foot. 'Put your torch on,' she called to Philip. 'We might be able to sleep here.'

It proved to be a small cave, with a soft, dry sandy floor. It smelt a little of seaweed, but nobody minded that. They dragged their rugs in, and flung themselves down. Huffin and Puffin squatted at the opening of the cave, as if they had put themselves on guard.

Almost before their heads touched the rugs the boys were asleep. The girls followed suit, and soon there was nothing to be heard but tiny snores from Jack, who was flat on his back. Kiki examined his face in the darkness to find out why her beloved Jack was making such queer little noises, then decided they weren't worth bothering about. She sat herself down in the middle of his tummy and went to sleep too.

The next morning Huffin and Puffin walked over to Philip and stood heavily on him. 'Arrrr!' they said, meaning 'Come on, wake up!'

Philip awoke. 'Get off,' he said. 'Don't copy Kiki's bad ways, Huffin and Puffin. Oh, I say – thanks for the fish – but don't put them all over my chest, Huffin!'

Huffin had been diving for fish. He now deposited them carefully on Philip, opened and shut his mouth a few times, and made his one and only remark, in a deep and satisfied voice. 'Arrrrrrrrrrr!'

The children laughed when they heard about Huffin's morning offering. They rubbed their eyes and decided to have a dip in the sea, for they all felt dirty.

'Then we'll have breakfast,' said Jack. 'Gosh, I wish I wasn't always so frightfully hungry. I say, this is rather a nice island, isn't it? Look, you can see the enemy's island on the horizon over there. Wonder if Bill is there.'

'We'll go up to the highest point on this island after breakfast, and have a good look round at all the others,' said Philip. 'Let's go and get some food from the boat.'

The boat was afloat on the high tide. The children had to swim out to her. They rifled her for food – and whilst she was looking for a tin of salmon she knew she had put in, Lucy-Ann found something that made her shout.

'I say, look! – a wireless! Do you suppose it is a transmitter as well as a receiver? Can we send a message on it?'

'Don't know,' said Jack, examining it. 'It's not a bit like Bill's. If only we knew! Anyway, even if we *could* send out messages on it, I wouldn't know how to. I expect it's just some sort of portable wireless. Come on, let's have breakfast. Phew, this sun's hot.'

With Huffin, Puffin, Kiki and the three rats all sharing their breakfast, the four children made a very good meal on the boat. 'Now, what next?' said Jack. 'Shall we go up to the topmost height in this island and see what's all round us?'

'Yes,' said the others, so, leaving the boat by itself, they made their way up the low cliff and on to the grass-grown land behind. It was not so heathery as Puffin Island had been, nor were there many birds on it.

'It's funny. You'd think there would be plenty on a nice little island like this,' said Jack. 'Look, there's a hill at the other end of the island! – let's climb it.'

They climbed to the very top – and then they stood still in astonishment. Beyond them, sparkling blue, was a lagoon, flat and still as a mirror. It lay between two islands, but the islands were joined by broad strips of rocks that enclosed the whole lagoon, so that it was impossible to say which island it really belonged to. The rocks ran out from each one, in some places as high as cliffs – and there between them lay this unbelievably lovely sea-lake.

'Look at that!' said Jack in awe. 'We've seen some wonderful sights – but never one as beautiful as that blue lagoon. It can't be real.'

But it was. It stretched out below them for about a mile and a half, so sheltered and protected that not a ripple broke its calm blue surface.

And then something happened that gave the children a shock of amazement. They heard the low hum of an aeroplane. They saw it coming towards them. Jack pulled them down flat in case they were seen. It flew right over the lagoon, and as it flew, something dropped from it – something that opened out, billowed white, and had something else fixed below it.

The children watched in amazement. All sorts of ridiculous things flashed through their minds – was it a scientific experiment – bombs – atom bombs – what was it?

A little parachute had opened, and was swinging down to the lagoon. The package underneath it was wrapped in glistening stuff – some kind of waterproof material, Jack thought. It reached the water and disappeared. The parachute spread itself out on the calm surface and lay still. But as the children watched, it seemed to dissolve and finally it too disappeared into the water.

'Look – the plane is circling the lagoon again. It's going to drop another,' said Philip. They all watched as the plane once more dropped a parachute, and the same thing happened.

Down to the water it floated with its unknown package, and in a few minutes all trace of it had disappeared. A third one was sent down and then the aeroplane circled round once and headed away. Soon it was lost in the distance.

'Well, whatever in the world was it doing, dropping things into this lagoon?' said Jack in astonishment. 'What a strange thing to do! What's in those enormous packages the parachutes carry?'

'And why drop them into the lagoon?' wondered Dinah. 'It seems so silly. Do they want to get rid of something? What a strange way to do it!'

'Let's take the boat and go and sail over the lagoon to see if we can see down into the depths,' said Lucy-Ann.

'And how do you think we are going to get *in*to the lagoon, idiot?' said Jack. 'No boat can get into that water – unless it's dragged over that barrier of rocks surrounding it.'

'Yes – of course – how silly of me!' said Lucy-Ann. 'I do wish we could see down into that water though – and find out what secrets it is holding, down in the blue depths.'

'Arrrrr!' said Huffin and Puffin, and, their wings vibrating quickly, they sailed down to the lagoon as if to say 'You want to go there? Well, it's easy.'

They bobbed there on the lagoon, very small specks indeed, diving under the water for fish. The children watched them.

'I don't see why we can't go and have a bathe there,' said Jack at last. 'We could swim a good way out and then dive down to see if we could find out anything. You never know!'

'Well, let's go now then,' said Dinah eagerly. 'I feel as if I simply *must* find out what all this is about. It's the most peculiar secret, I must say!'

They began to scramble down the hill. It grew rocky as they got lower down, but there were plenty of sea-pink cushions to soften the way for their feet. At last they reached the edge of the calm blue water.

They undressed and went in. The water was very warm indeed, and rippled like soft silk over their arms. They swam out slowly, enjoying the warmth of the lake and of the sun on their shoulders.

'Now I'm going to dive down and see if I can make out anything,' said Jack, and turning himself up like a duck, down he went, down and down and down. What would he find at the bottom?

Chapter 24
An amazing discovery

The lagoon was quite deep. Jack could not swim to the bottom, because he couldn't possibly hold his breath long enough. He came up, gasping.

'All I could see was a pile of silvery stuff lying on the bottom,' he gasped to the others. 'Nothing else at all. I couldn't go right down to it, because I hadn't enough breath.'

'Well, that's not much use,' said Dinah. 'We want to see what's *inside* the waterproof wrapping – tear it off, so that we can see what it holds.'

'We wouldn't be able to do that very easily,' said Philip. 'I bet it's sewn up pretty tightly – or sealed in some clever way. I'll go down, Jack – perhaps I can get near enough to *feel* what's inside.'

'Oh dear – do be careful,' said Lucy-Ann. 'You don't know *what* might be inside!'

'Well – it's hardly likely to be anything that will eat us,' grinned Jack. 'Kiki, why don't *you* do a little diving, like Huffin and Puffin do — you could be a bit of help then!'

But Kiki did not approve of all this love of bathing. She flew about above the children in the water and tried occasionally to perch on a bare shoulder. Huffin and Puffin loved having the children in the water, and swam and dived beside them, uttering deep *arrrrrs* of satisfaction.

Philip dived under, and swam rapidly downwards, his eyes wide open in the salt water. Far below him he saw the silvery mass, gleaming dimly on the lagoon bed. He swam right down to it, and put out his hand to touch it. Beneath the wrapping he felt something very hard indeed.

Then, his breath giving out, he rose up to the surface, almost bursting. He took in great gulps of air.

'I felt something hard,' he said at last. 'But it was impossible to tell what it was. Blow! Isn't it sickening to be right on top of a mystery like this, and not be able to solve it?'

'We shall have to give it up,' said Jack. 'I know perfectly well I haven't enough breath to go down and probe the wrappings. I should burst for want of breath.'

'I do hate giving things up,' said Dinah.

'Well, swim under the water yourself and see if *you* can find out anything,' said Philip.

'You know I can't hold my breath even as long as you can,' said Dinah. 'So what's the good of that?'

'I'm going to swim back to shore,' said Lucy-Ann. 'There's a nice sunny rock over there, covered with seaweed. I shall have a sunbathe there.'

She swam slowly over to it. Huffin and Puffin dived under, just beside her. 'I wonder what they look like when they swim under water,' thought Lucy-Ann. 'I'd love to see them chasing a fish.'

She turned herself up, and duck-dived under the water. Ah, there was Huffin, using his wings to swim swiftly through the water after a big fish. Quick, Huffin, or you'll lose it!

Just as she was going to swim upwards again Lucy-Ann noticed something below her. The lagoon was not nearly so deep just there, for a shelf of rocks ran out into the water, making it fairly shallow, although it was much too deep still for Lucy-Ann's feet to touch the bottom.

The little girl took a quick glance to see what it was on the rocks below the water, but then her breath gave out, and, half choking, she rose up to the surface, gasping and spluttering.

When she had got her breath again, down she went – and then she realised what it was she saw. One of the parachuted packages, instead of falling into the deeper waters of the lagoon, had fallen on to the shallow rocky bed just below her. The package had split open – and all its contents were spread and scattered on the rocky bottom below.

But whatever were they? Lucy-Ann could not make them out at all. They looked such peculiar shapes. She rose up to the surface again and yelled to Jack.

'Hi, Jack! One of those secret packages has split open on the rocky bottom just here – but I can't make out what was in it!'

The boys and Dinah swam up in great excitement. They all duck-dived and down they went, down, down, down. They came to where the silvery wrapping was split open, moving gently up and down with the flow of the water. All around it were the spilt contents.

The boys, almost bursting for breath, examined them quickly, then shot up to the surface, gasping.

They looked at one another, and then both shouted the same words.

'Guns! Guns! Scores of them!'

The children swam to the sunny rock that Lucy-Ann was

now sitting on, and clambered up.

'Fancy that! Guns! What in the wide world do they want to drop guns down in this lagoon for? Are they getting rid of them? And why?'

'No. They wouldn't wrap them up so carefully in water-proof stuff if they were just dumping them,' said Philip soberly. 'They're hiding them.'

'*Hiding* them! But what a very peculiar place to hide guns in!' said Dinah. 'What are they going to do with them?'

'They're probably gun-running,' said Jack, 'bringing hundreds of guns here from somewhere, and hiding them till they're ready for them – ready for some revolution somewhere – South America, perhaps.'

'Something like that, I bet,' said Philip. 'There are always people stirring up trouble *some*where, and wanting weapons to fight with. Those who can supply them with guns would make a lot of money. Yes, that's what it is – gun-running!'

'*Well!*' said Lucy-Ann, 'to think we've dropped right into an awful thing like that! I expect Bill guessed it – and they saw him snooping round – and captured him so that he couldn't give the game away.'

'However do they get the guns away from here?' wondered Jack. 'I mean – they can't be got away by boat, because this lagoon is absolutely enclosed by rocks. Yet the guns must be taken out of the water, to be sent to wherever they are wanted. It's jolly queer.'

'Well, now we *do* know what that aeroplane was dropping,' said Philip. 'My word – this lagoon must be full of arma-ments! What an absolutely wonderful hiding-place – nobody to see what happens, nobody to discover the guns at the bottom . . .'

'Except us,' said Lucy-Ann promptly. '*I* discovered that split package. I suppose it hit the rocks just below the surface and split open at once.'

They lay basking in the sun, talking over the curious

discovery. Then Kiki suddenly uttered an astonished cry, and the children sat up to see why.

'Goodness – there's a boat coming,' said Jack in dismay. 'Coming towards this very place, too, from the seaward side of the rocky barrier.'

'What shall we do?' said Lucy-Ann, frightened. 'There's nowhere to hide, and we haven't time to make our way back without being seen.'

The boys gazed round in desperation. What could be done? Then Philip suddenly grabbed up a great armful of seaweed and flung it over the surprised Lucy-Ann.

'We'll cover ourselves up with this!' he said. 'There's stacks of it! Quick! Pull it up and cover yourselves with it. It's the only way we can hide.'

Their hearts thumping loudly again, the four children piled the thickly growing seaweed, with its great ribbon-like fronds, all over themselves. Jack peered through his and spoke urgently to Dinah.

'One of your feet is showing, Di. Put some seaweed over it, quick!'

Huffin and Puffin were amazed at this sudden seaweed game. They decided which lump was Philip and went to perch solemnly on him. He felt their weight, and almost laughed.

'Nobody could possibly guess there was a boy under these two puffins and all the seaweed,' he thought. 'I only hope the others are really well covered.'

The boat grounded not far off. The voices of two or three men could be heard, coming nearer and nearer. The children held their breath. 'Don't tread on us, oh, don't tread on us!' prayed Lucy-Ann, feeling quite sick, especially as there was a great flabby piece of seaweed across her mouth.

The men did not tread on them. They came and stood quite nearby, however, and all of them lighted cigarettes as they stood there.

'The last lot of stuff came today,' said one man, in a husky, deep voice. 'This lagoon must be almost full now.'

'Yes. Time we got some of it away,' said another voice, a sharp, commanding kind of voice. 'We don't know how much information that fellow we've got has passed on to his headquarters. He won't talk. Better send a message through to the chief, to tell him to collect as much as he wants, in case anyone else is sent along to snoop.'

'What about the second fellow? He won't talk either,' said the first voice. 'What are we going to do with them?'

'They can't remain up here,' said the commanding voice. 'Put them on the boat tonight, and we'll dump them somewhere where they won't be heard of again. I'm not going to waste my time on that first fellow any more – what's his name? – Cunningham. He's been enough trouble to us, poking his noise into all we do for the last year. Time he disappeared.'

The four hidden children, feeling very damp and cold under their seaweed, shivered to hear all this. They knew perfectly well what was meant. They, these men, were Bill's bitter enemies, because he had been successful in keeping on their track – now they had got him, and they were afraid he knew too much, though actually it was likely that Bill didn't know as much as they, the children, did.

'And so they are going to remove all these guns and then dump poor Bill somewhere so that he never *will* be heard of again, because he will be drowned,' thought Jack desperately. 'We shall *have* to rescue him. And as quickly as possible too. I wonder who the other fellow is they are talking about. Surely it can't be Horace. I thought he was one of the enemy.'

The men wandered away over the rocks. Evidently they had come to survey their extraordinary hiding-place though they could see very little of its contents. The children lay perfectly still, not daring to move, in case they should be noticed. They got very tired indeed of lying there, and Lucy-Ann was shivering.

Then they heard the sound of the motor-boat's engine starting up again. Thank goodness! They waited a while, and then Jack sat cautiously up. He looked round. There was no-one to be seen. The men had gone back to the boat by a different way, and it was now some distance out to sea.

'Phew!' said Jack. 'I didn't like that at all. Another inch or two nearer, and one of the men would have trodden on my foot!'

Chapter 25
Another surprise

They all sat up and removed the slippery seaweed from themselves. Huffin and Puffin walked down Philip's body, where they had perched the whole time. Kiki, to her fright and dismay, had been covered with seaweed by Jack, and forced to stay beside him, for he was afraid she might give them away by talking. She talked angrily now.

'Poor, poor Polly! Send for the doctor! What a pity, what a pity, ding dong bell, Polly's in the well!'

The children looked at one another solemnly when they had finished uncovering themselves. Bill was in great danger, there was no doubt of that at all.

'What are we going to do?' said Lucy-Ann, with tears in her eyes. Nobody quite knew. There seemed to be danger wherever they turned.

'Well,' said Jack at last, 'we've got a boat of our own, that's one thing – and I think when it's dark tonight we'd better set out for the other island, the one the men are on, and see if we can't find where they keep their motor-boat. We know that Bill will be there.'

'And rescue him!' said Dinah, thrilled. 'But how shall we get close in to shore without being seen or heard?'

'We'll go when it's dark, as I said,' said Jack, 'and when we get near to the shore, we'll stop our engine and get the oars. Then we can row in without being heard '

'Oh yes. I'd forgotten there were oars in our boat,' said Dinah. 'Thank goodness!'

'Can't we get back to our little cave, on the shore at the other side of the island?' asked Lucy-Ann. 'I don't feel safe here, somehow. And I'd be glad to know our boat was all right.'

'Also, we can't have anything to eat till we get back there,' said Philip, getting up. 'Come on, I'm frozen. We shall get warm climbing up the rocks, on to the height over there, and then over the island to the boat.'

So they went back over the rocks, and found their clothes where they had left them. They stripped off their wet suits and dressed quickly. Philip's rats, which he had left in his pockets, were extremely pleased to see him again, and ran all over him with little squeals of delight.

Huffin and Puffin accompanied the children as usual. All of them were secretly relieved to find their boat was safe on the shingly beach. They went to her and chose some tins of food.

'Better have something with lots of juice to drink,' said Jack. 'There's no fresh water here as far as I can see, and I'm awfully thirsty. Let's open a tin of pineapple. There's always lots of juice in that.'

'Better open *two* tins if Kiki's going to have any,' said Dinah. 'You know what a pig she is over pineapple.'

They all tried to be jolly and cheerful, but somehow, what with their strange discovery of the guns in the lagoon, and the news that Bill was in real danger, none of them could talk for long. One by one they fell silent, and hardly knew what they were eating.

'I suppose,' said Dinah at last, after a long silence in which the only noise was the sound of Kiki's beak scraping against the bottom of one of the pineapple tins, 'I suppose we had better set out as soon as it's dark – but I do feel quaky about it!'

'Well, look here,' said Jack, 'I've been thinking hard –

and I'm sure it would be best if Philip and I went alone to get Bill. It's very risky, and we don't know a bit what we shall be up against, and I don't like the idea of you girls coming.'

'Oh, we *must* come!' cried Lucy-Ann, who couldn't bear the thought of Jack going off without her. 'Supposing something happened to you – we'd be here on this island all alone, and nobody would know about us! Anyway, I'm going with you, Jack. You can't stop me!'

'All right,' said Jack. 'Perhaps it would be better if we stuck together. I say – I suppose that other fellow they spoke about couldn't be Horace? We couldn't have made a mistake about him, could we?'

'Well, I did think he was too idiotic for words,' said Dinah. 'I mean – he *looked* it, not only acted it. I believe we did make a mistake. I think perhaps he really was a bird-lover.'

'Gosh! He must have thought we were frightful!' said Jack, horrified. 'And we took his boat too – and left him to be taken prisoner by the enemy!'

'And they must have thought he was Bill's friend, and have been wild with him when he said he didn't know Bill or anything about him,' said Philip.

Everyone thought solemnly about poor Horace. 'I'm jolly glad none of us hit him on the head, after all,' said Jack. 'Poor old Horace Tripalong!'

'We'll have to rescue him, too,' said Lucy-Ann. 'That'll make up a bit for taking his boat. But won't he be *furious* with us for all we've done!'

Huffin appeared at this moment with his familiar gift of half a dozen fish, neatly arranged head and tail alternately in his large beak. He deposited them at Philip's feet.

'Thanks, old man,' said Philip. 'But won't you eat them yourself? We daren't make a fire here to cook anything on.'

'Arrrrr!' said Huffin, and walked over to have a look in the empty tins. Puffin took the opportunity of gobbling up the fish, and Kiki watched her in disgust. Kiki had no use for fish fresh from the sea.

'Pah!' she said, in Horace's voice, and the children smiled.

'Kiki, you'll have to be jolly quiet tonight,' said Jack, scratching her head. 'No pahing or poohing to warn the enemy we're near!'

When the sun began to sink the children took the motor-boat a little way out to sea, to make sure that there were no rocks about that they must avoid when setting out at night. Far away on the horizon line they saw the island of the enemy. Somewhere there was Bill – and perhaps Horace too.

'I hope to goodness we see some kind of light to show us where to go inshore,' said Jack. 'We can't go all round the island, looking for the right place. We'd be heard. And we couldn't possibly row round.'

'Well, we saw that light that was signalling to the other boat last night,' said Philip. 'Maybe it will be signalling again. Let's go back now. There doesn't seem to be any rock to avoid tonight. We'll set out as soon as it is dark.'

They went back – and no sooner had they got to their little beach than they heard the humming of an aeroplane.

'Surely they're not going to drop any more packages!' said Jack. 'Lie down flat, all of you. We don't want to be spotted. Get near those rocks.'

They crouched down near a mass of rocks. The aeroplane made an enormous noise as it came nearer and nearer.

Jack gave a cry. 'It's a seaplane! Look, it's got floats underneath!'

'What an enormous one!' said Dinah. 'It's coming down!'

So it was. It circled the island once and then came lower as it circled it again. It seemed almost to brush the hill that towered at the other end of the island, the hill that over-looked the lagoon.

Then the engines were cut out, and there was a silence.

'She's landed,' said Jack. 'She's on the lagoon! I bet you

anything you like that's where she is!'

'Oh, do let's go and see, as soon as dusk comes,' begged Dinah. 'Do you think she's going to get up the hidden guns?'

'However could she do that?' said Jack, rather scornfully.

'Well, she's pretty big and hefty,' said Philip. 'It's possible she's got some sort of apparatus on her for dragging up the hidden armaments. If the men think there's a danger of our Government sending patrols up here to look into the matter, always supposing that Bill has sent a message through to his headquarters, then our enemy will certainly try to remove the guns as soon as possible. It rather looks, seeing that this is a seaplane, as if the guns are going to be flown to South America – or somewhere far across the sea.'

As soon as it was dusk the children could not resist the temptation to go across the island and climb up the heights to peep over and see the lagoon. Even in the twilight they might be able to see something interesting.

They were soon on the cliff overlooking the lagoon. They could just make out the great shape of the giant seaplane in the middle of the sea-lake. Then suddenly lights shone out from it, and a noise began – a grating, dragging noise, as if some kind of machinery was being set to do some heavy work.

'I bet they're dragging up the packages of guns,' whispered Jack. 'We can't very well see – but we can hear enough to know something is at work, something needing winches, I should think.'

Lucy-Ann didn't know what winches were, but she could quite well imagine some kind of machinery that would send hooked cables overboard to drag up the heavy bundles of guns. Then the seaplane, when loaded up, would fly off again. And another would come, and another! Or maybe the same one would come back again and again.

The lights showed the children the vast shape of the seaplane. It looked weird lying quietly there in the middle of the dark lagoon. Lucy-Ann shivered.

'It's awful to be up against enemies who have boats and aeroplanes and seaplanes and guns,' she thought. 'We haven't anything except poor Horace's little motor-boat, and our own wits.'

They went back soberly to their boat. The tide had taken it out a little way, but as they had tied a rope to a convenient rock, they pulled it in without difficulty. They all got on board.

'Now this is the greatest adventure of all,' said Jack, rather solemnly. 'Hiding is an adventure. Escaping is an adventure. But rescuing somebody else from the very jaws of the enemy is the greatest adventure of all.'

'If only we don't get captured ourselves!' said Lucy-Ann.

Jack started up the engine. The little boat nosed out to sea, leaving the lagoon island behind. Huffin and Puffin settled themselves on the deck-rail as usual, and Kiki sat on Jack's shoulder. Philip's rats, frightened at the sudden noise of the engine, twined themselves together in a large bump in the hollow of Philip's back. 'You tickle me!' he said, but the rats took no notice.

'Well, good luck to us all!' said Dinah. 'May we rescue Bill – and Horace too – defeat the enemy – and get back home in safety!'

'God save the King!' said Kiki devoutly, in exactly the same tone of voice, and everyone laughed. Funny old Kiki!

Chapter 26
Off to the enemy's island

The little boat sped along in the darkness. Philip was at the wheel. He took a large star as guide, and kept the boat well on its course.

After a while Jack touched his arm. 'See that light? It must come from the enemy's island. It's not the bright signalling light we saw before, but it certainly comes from the island.'

'I'll set course for it,' said Philip. 'You'll make certain Kiki doesn't go off into one of her cackles or screeches, won't you, Jack? Any noise out here on the water would be easily heard on land. Sound over water carries such a distance. I'll have to shut off the engine soon, or that will be heard.'

'Kiki won't make a sound,' said Jack.

'Shhhhhhh!' said Kiki at once.

'Yes. Good bird! Shhhhhhh!' said Jack. Philip shut off the engine and the boat gradually lost way until it was just drifting on. Then it came to a gentle stop on the restless sea.

Jack looked through his glasses at the light he could see on the island. 'I think it must be some sort of harbour light,' he said. 'Perhaps they have a small harbour there – they may have quite a fleet of motor-boats, you know, continually patrolling to make sure no-one visits islands near here. It's quite a steady light.'

Philip fumbled for the oars. 'Now for a spot of hard rowing!' he said. 'What's the time, Jack? Can you see by your wrist-watch? It's got a luminous face, hasn't it?'

'It's almost eleven o'clock,' said Jack. 'Just about right. We shall be nearing land about midnight, when we can hope that the enemy won't be wide awake.'

The boys took an oar each. Splish-splash! the oars went in and out of the water as the boys pulled with a will, and the boat glided smoothly along.

'We'll take turns when you're tired,' said Dinah. 'Philip, where are your rats? Something brushed against my leg just now. I shan't be able to help squealing if you let them run about.'

'They're in my pocket,' said Philip. 'You're imagining things, as usual. And if you dare to squeal, I'll jolly well tip you overboard!'

'She won't, she won't,' said Lucy-Ann. 'It's only Huffin

and Puffin walking about the deck, Dinah. One of them perched on my leg just now.'

'Arrrr!' said a guttural voice from the deck-rail.

'Shhhhhh!' said Kiki at once.

'She doesn't understand that it doesn't in the least matter Huffin and Puffin *arrr*ing all they like,' said Jack. 'They make a natural bird-noise that wouldn't put anyone on guard.'

'Shhhhhh!' said Kiki reprovingly.

The light from the shore gleamed steadily. 'Must be from a lantern,' said Jack, in a low voice, pulling hard at his oar. 'Probably a guide to any motor-boat going in or out. Philip, let's have a rest. I'm getting puffed.'

'Right,' said Philip. The girls wanted to take a turn, but Jack wouldn't let them. 'No, you don't row as well together as Philip and I do. We can keep having a rest if we want to. There's no hurry. The later we are the better, in a way.'

They soon took the oars again, and their boat moved steadily over the water towards the light.

'No more talking now,' whispered Jack. 'Only tiny whispers.'

Lucy-Ann's knees went queer again. Her tummy felt peculiar too. Dinah was strung up and her breath came fast, although she was not rowing. The two boys were tense with excitement. Would they find the enemy's motor-boat there, with Bill already in it, ready to be 'dumped,' as the man had said that day? And would there be many men on guard?

'Whatever's that noise?' whispered Dinah at last, as their boat drew nearer to land. 'It does sound queer.'

The boys paused in their rowing, and leaned on their oars to listen.

'Sounds like a band playing,' said Jack. 'Of course – it's a wireless!'

'Good!' said Philip. 'Then the enemy won't be so likely to hear us creeping in. Jack, look! – I think that's a little jetty there – you can just make it out by the light of that lantern. Can we possibly creep in without being seen or heard? And look! – is that a boat lying under the lantern?'

'I'll get the glasses,' said Philip, and felt about for them. He put them to his eyes. 'Yes – it *is* a boat – quite a big one. I should think it's the one the enemy came to our island in. I bet Bill is on it, battened down in the cabin!'

The band continued playing on the wireless. 'Somebody on board has got it on,' said Jack. 'The guard, I should think. Will he be on deck, then – the guard, I mean? There's no light there.'

'If you ask me, he's having a nice lazy time, snoozing on deck with his wireless playing him nice tunes,' whispered back Philip. 'Look! – can you see that little glow, Jack? I bet that's the end of a cigarette the guard is smoking.'

'Yes, it probably is,' said Jack.

'I don't think we dare go in any closer,' said Philip. 'We don't want to be seen. If the guard gives the alarm, we're done for. I wonder how many there are on the deck. I can only see one glowing cigarette-end.'

'What are you going to do?' whispered Lucy-Ann. 'Do do something. I feel awful! I shall burst in a minute.'

Philip put out his hand and took hers. 'Don't worry,' he whispered. 'We shall have to do something soon! It looks to be rather a good time. If only that guard would fall asleep!'

'I say, Tufty – do you know what I think would be much the best thing to do?' said Jack suddenly. 'If you and I swam to the harbour, climbed up, got on the boat and surprised the guard, we could probably tip him into the water, and before he could raise the alarm, we'd open up the hatch and get Bill out. Why, we could probably drive the motor-boat off too – then we'd have two!'

'Sounds a good plan,' said Philip. 'But we don't know yet if Bill is there – and it's quite likely we couldn't tip the guard overboard – especially if there are more than one. We'd better do a little exploring first. Your idea of slipping overboard and swimming to the harbour is jolly good though. We'll certainly do that. We can clamber up a part where there are shadows, away from that light.'

'Oh dear – must you go swimming in the dark?' said Lucy-Ann, looking at the black water with a shiver. 'I should hate it. Do, do be careful, Jack!'

'I'll be all right,' said Jack. 'Come on, Philip. Strip off your clothes. We'll swim in our pants.'

It wasn't long before the boys silently slid overboard and entered the water. It was cold and they drew their breaths in sharply. But they soon felt warm as they swam rapidly towards the harbour. They could hear the wireless more plainly as they came near. 'Good thing,' thought Jack. 'They won't be able to hear us coming at all.'

They avoided the light, and clambered up the part of the jetty where there were black shadows. It was not easy. 'The boat's just there,' whispered Jack in Philip's ear. 'Not right under the light, thank goodness!'

A sound made them stop suddenly. A loud and prolonged yawn came from the deck of the boat. Then the wireless was snapped off and silence came back to the night.

'He may be going to sleep,' hissed Jack. 'Let's wait.'

They waited in complete silence for about ten minutes. The man tossed a glowing cigarette-end overboard but did not light another. The boys heard him give several grunts as if he was settling down comfortably. Then he gave a loud yawn again.

Still the boys waited, shivering in the darkness of the jetty, keeping close to one another in order to get a little bit of warmth from each other's bodies.

Then, on the night air, came very very welcome sounds. 'He's snoring,' whispered Jack, pressing Philip's arm in joy. 'He's asleep. I'm sure there's only one guard, because other-wise they would have been talking together. Now's our chance. Come on – but quietly, so as not to wake him!'

The two boys, shivering now with excitement as much as with cold, crept along the jetty to the boat. They climbed cautiously on board, their bare feet making no sound at all.

On the deck lay the sleeping guard – if he was a guard!

Then another sound stopped them. This time it came from beneath their feet. Philip clutched Jack's bare arm and made him jump violently. They stood and listened.

It was somebody talking, down below in the cabin. Who was it? Could it be Bill? And who was he with? Horace perhaps. But maybe after all it wasn't Bill down there, maybe it was the enemy, playing cards, and perhaps the sleeping man wasn't a guard. It would be very foolish to toss him overboard and open the cabin hatch to find the enemy down in the cabin.

'We'd better listen and find out if it's Bill,' said Jack, right in Philip's ear. The boys could see thin streaks of light where the hatch was fitted down into the deck, covering in the little cabin; so they knew exactly where it was. They crept forward and then knelt down by the closed hatch. They put their ears to the cracks and strained to listen to the voices talking.

They could not hear what was being said – but, when one of the talkers suddenly cleared his throat and gave a little cough, the boys knew who it was all right! It was one of Bill's little ways. Bill was down there. It was Bill who was talking. Both boys felt a surge of tremendous relief. If only they could get Bill out, and let him take charge of things!

'If we throw this fellow overboard, we may find he raises the alarm so quickly that we shan't be able to get Bill out and explain things to him fast enough,' said Jack, in Philip's ear. 'As he's so fast asleep, what about unbolting the hatch and letting Bill see we're here? Then he could help us with the guard, and take charge of the boat.'

'You undo the hatch, and I'll stand by the guard, so that if he wakes I can knock him overboard,' said Philip. 'Go on. Quick!'

Jack felt for the bolt. His fingers were trembling and he could hardly pull it. He was afraid it might make a grating noise, but it didn't. It slid back easily and smoothly. Jack felt for the iron handle that raised the hatch, and then lifted up the hatch itself, so that a bright mass of light came up from the cabin below.

The men in the cabin heard the slight noise and looked up. One was Bill – and the other was Horace. When Bill saw Jack's face peering down out of the darkness he leapt to his feet in amazement. Jack put his finger to his lips, and Bill bit back the exclamation on his tongue.

'Come on out,' whispered Jack. 'Quick! We've got to deal with the guard here.'

But Horace spoilt everything. As soon as he saw Jack, the hated boy who had shut him into the hole on Puffin Island, he sprang up furiously. 'There's that villainous boy! Wait till I get him!' he shouted.

Chapter 27
Escape

'Sh!' said Jack fiercely, and pointed over his shoulder towards the guard. But it was too late. The man awoke with a jump, as the shouting penetrated into his dreams. He sat up blinking, and then, seeing the brilliant light streaming up from the open hatch, he leapt to his feet.

Bill had the sense to switch off the light. Now all was darkness. Bill began to climb up the hatchway, and the guard began to shout.

'What's all this? Hi, what are you doing? Who's there?'

Philip sprang at him and tried to push him overboard, but the man was strong and began to struggle. In the end it was poor Philip who was thrown overboard, with a most terrific splash. Then Bill came up and, guided by the sound of the panting of the guard, hit out with his right fist. The surprised guard felt the sudden blow and reeled over. Bill put out a foot, hoping to trip him, and down he went to the deck. In a trice Bill was on top of him, and Jack came

to help. 'Who was that going overboard?' panted Bill.

'Philip,' answered Jack, sitting firmly on the guard's legs. 'He's all right. He can swim to the other boat.'

'Get the guard down into the cabin,' ordered Bill. 'Where's the other fellow – Tipperlong? The idiot spoilt the whole show.'

Horace was standing well out of the way, wondering what was happening. He could hear pants and groans and strugglings, and he was scared. Then there came another yell from the guard, and down the man went into the cabin, slithering sideways down the steps.

Bang! The hatch shut down on him and Bill slid the bolt across.

'He's safe for the moment,' said Bill grimly. 'Now let's get the boat going, quick! We'll be off before the enemy know what we're up to!'

'That's what I planned we'd do!' panted Jack, thrilled

that his wildest hopes seemed to be coming true. 'How do we start up the engine? Blow this darkness! I haven't a torch on me.'

The guard below was kicking up a terrific row. He was yelling and banging for all he was worth. Bill made his way in the darkness to the wheel of the boat.

And then things began to happen. Lights sprang up on shore, and voices began to shout. There came the sound of running feet.

'We shan't have time to get her free from her moorings and start her up before they're on us,' groaned Bill. 'Did you say you've got another boat here, Jack? Where is it? And what about Philip? Quick, answer me!'

'Yes – there's a boat off the end of the jetty there – with the girls in it – and Philip will probably be there by now, too,' said Jack, his words falling over one another in his excitement. 'We'd better swim for it!'

'Overboard then!' said Bill. 'Tipperlong, where are you? You'd better come too.'

'I c-c-c-can't swim,' stammered poor Horace.

'Well, jump overboard and I'll help you,' commanded Bill. But the thought of leaping into the dark cold water in the middle of the night, with enemies all round, was too much for Horace. He crawled into a corner and refused to move.

'Well, stay where you are, then,' said Bill scornfully. 'I'll have to go with these kids – can't let them down now!'

Overboard went Bill and Jack. Horace heard the splashes and shivered. Nothing would have induced him to do the same. He trembled in his corner, waiting for the enemy to come pounding down the jetty.

And come they did, with torches flashing, and voices that urgently demanded from the guard what all the noise was about. They swarmed on board the motor-boat, and found Horace at once, shivering in the corner. They dragged him out.

The guard was still hammering down in the cabin, getting hoarse with fury. The enemy, not really certain of what had happened, flung questions at poor Horace.

Bill and Jack, swimming swiftly through the dark water, heard the excited voices, and prayed that Horace would not give them away. The guard would soon tell them all they wanted to know, but perhaps the few minutes' start they had would be all they needed.

Philip was already on board the boat, reassuring the two frightened girls. When he heard the splash of Bill and Jack jumping overboard from the other boat, he strained his eyes to watch for them. As he caught the sound of their swift armstrokes through the water, he cautiously held his torch down over the sea, and flicked it on once or twice, to mark their way for them.

They saw the slight flashes of light and thankfully swam towards them. Jack had been afraid of missing the boat altogether in his excitement. Soon they were clambering up, and Lucy-Ann and Dinah caught hold of Bill's wet, hairy arms, so strong and firm and comforting.

'Come on – we must get going,' said Bill, giving each girl a quick pat. 'My, what a row there is on that boat! They've let the guard out now. Come on, before they know where we are.'

'The engine will tell them, when we start it up,' said Jack. 'We've got oars. Shall we row?'

'No,' said Bill. 'We must get away as quickly as possible. They'll chase us, and we *must* get a good start. You girls lie flat on your tummies, and you boys lie on top of them. There'll be bullets flying after me in a tick!'

Bill started up the engine. Lucy-Ann and Dinah lay down flat. The boys lay on top of them, almost squeezing the breath out of the girls. It was most uncomfortable.

Queerly enough not one of the children felt frightened. They all felt a terrific excitement, and Lucy-Ann had a mad feeling that she would like to yell and dance about. It was hard to have to keep flat on the deck, with Jack squashing her breath out of her.

As soon as the engine of the motor-boat started up, there came an astonished silence on board the other boat. Plainly the guard had not gathered that there was a second boat not far off, and had not told his friends about it. The enemy had thought that Bill and his rescuers were swimming somewhere about, and they were still quite in the dark about what had happened.

But when the engine of Bill's (or rather Horace's) boat purred out in the night, the enemy knew that they must stop it somehow. That boat could not be allowed to get away!

Crack! Somebody's revolver went off, and a bullet sped over the sea, towards the boat.

Crack! Crack! Crack! Bill crouched as low as he could by the wheel, as he heard a bullet whizz much too near the boat for his liking.

'Keep down, you kids!' he ordered anxiously. 'We'll soon be out of reach.'

Crack! Another bullet went pinging by, and struck the water beyond the boat. Bill said several things under his breath, and wished the motor-boat would go a little faster.

R-r-r-r-r-r-r went the engine steadily, and the boat swung over the waves out to sea.

Crack! Crack!

There came a sudden squeal from Kiki, who was sitting on top of Jack, puzzled by all the noise and excitement. Then she screeched wildly.

'Oh! Kiki's hit!' shouted Jack, and sat up in anxiety, feeling for his beloved parrot.

Kiki didn't say a single word, but continued to screech as if she was in the most terrible pain. Jack was beside himself with grief.

'Keep down, you idiot!' roared Bill, sensing that Jack was not lying flat. 'Do you hear what I say?'

'But Kiki,' began Jack, only to be drowned by an even more furious roar from Bill.

'Kiki's all right! She couldn't screech like that if she was really hurt. Lie down flat, and do as you're told!'

Jack obeyed orders. He lay down again, and listened with anxiety to Kiki's screeching. The others, quite certain that the bird was wounded, were very anxious too.

Lucy-Ann wondered what had happened to Huffin and Puffin. She had not heard them say *arrrrr* for a long time. Perhaps they were shot too! Oh dear, when would they be out of reach of the enemy, and safe?

The shooting stopped – but another noise came, sounding faintly over the chugging of their own boat. Bill's sharp ears heard it.

'They're after us!' he called. 'They've started up their own boat. Thank goodness it's a dark night. We must just go on and on till our petrol gives out, and hope for the best.'

The motor-boat chasing them switched on a powerful searchlight. It swept the sea all round.

'We're just out of reach,' said Bill thankfully. 'This little boat can certainly get a move on. Kiki, shut up screeching! You're NOT hurt!'

'Bill, we might have enough petrol to get to the island

we came from, over to the east there,' said Jack suddenly. 'The men would probably think we'd try and make for safety miles away, and if we do, we shall certainly be overtaken. Their boat is more powerful than ours, and as soon as we get within the range of their searchlight, we'll be seen. Let's swing off to the left.'

'What island did you come from?' demanded Bill. 'And what's been happening to you all since I was fool enough to let myself get captured? I've been worrying my head off about you!'

'We were worried about you, too,' said Jack. 'Swing her to port, Bill – we'll make for the lagoon-island, and hope that the men won't guess we're there.'

The boat set course for the other island, across the dark, heaving sea. Far behind them the searchlight was still sweeping the waters, but it was plain that the enemy's motor-boat was now going off in the other direction. Another few minutes and they would be out of sight and hearing.

'Arrrrrrr!' said a guttural voice from just beyond Bill. He jumped. Then he laughed.

'My goodness – have you still got Huffin and Puffin? Now don't start screeching again, Kiki. I'm absolutely certain you're not hurt.'

'Can I sit up now and just *feel* if Kiki is hurt?' begged Jack anxiously. 'They're not doing any more shooting.'

But before Bill could answer, the engine of the motor-boat gave a series of coughs and wheezes, and then, with a curious sound like a tired sigh, stopped altogether.

'Petrol's run out,' said Bill bitterly. 'It would, of course! Now we'll have to row, and it won't be long before the enemy catch us up!'

Chapter 28
A night of talking

The children all sat up at once, and the girls thankfully stretched their arms and legs. 'You are heavy, Philip,' grumbled Dinah. 'Oh Bill – what awful bad luck to have no petrol just as we must be so near shore!'

Jack reached out for Kiki. His hands felt over her body anxiously, and down her legs, and over her beak. Where was she hurt?

Kiki nestled close to him, murmuring funny little words that had no sense. 'You're not hurt, silly bird,' said Jack thankfully. 'You made a fuss for nothing. I'm ashamed of you.'

'Poor Kiki, poor Kiki, send for the doctor,' murmured Kiki, and put her head under her wing.

'She's not hurt, as far as I can make out,' said Jack to the others, 'but she must have had an awful scare. Perhaps a bullet zipped very near her.'

'Oh, forget Kiki for a moment and let's talk about ourselves,' said Dinah. 'Bill, what are we going to do?'

Bill sat lost in thought. What was the best thing to do? It was no joke to be in charge of four children, with such dangerous enemies so near. Would it be best to make for this lagoon-island, whatever it was? It should at least be within rowing distance. Or would it be best to row further on?

'We'll make for your lagoon-island,' he said at last. 'It's the best idea.'

'It can't be far away,' said Jack, straining his eyes in the darkness. 'I think I can make out a dark shape over there. Can you, Philip?'

'Yes,' said Philip. 'Look, over there, Bill! Can you see?'

'Not a thing,' said Bill. 'But I'll take your word for it. You youngsters have got such sharp eyes and ears. Now, where are the oars?'

They were soon found, and the slow splish-splash of rowing came to the ears of the girls, as they sat huddled together for warmth.

'Yes – it *is* land of some sort,' said Bill, after a while, with satisfaction. 'We'll be ashore soon. I only hope there are no rocks to run aground on.'

'Oh no,' said Jack. 'We'll be all right. There aren't any rocks near the lagoon-island. At least, not the part where we should be coming to now.'

But hardly were the words out of his mouth before there came a horrid grinding noise, and the boat shivered from end to end. Everyone got a terrible shock. Whatever was happening now?

'On the rocks!' said Bill grimly. 'And I don't somehow think we'll get her off! She means to stay here all right!'

The boat could not be moved. Jack anxiously switched on a torch, and tried to see what had happened. It was only too plain!

'There are rocks all round,' he said dolefully. 'We haven't come to the right part of the island at all. Goodness knows where we are.'

'Let's see if we're holed,' said Bill, and took Jack's torch. He examined the boat thoroughly, and gave a sigh of relief. 'No. It looks as if we're safe so far. She must have run right on to a shallow ledge of rock. It's no use doing anything about it now. We'll have to wait till it's light and then see if we can shift her. If we mess about now and do get her off, we shall only get on to other rocks at once.'

'Well, let's snuggle down in rugs and have something to eat, and talk then,' said Lucy-Ann. 'I should never, never be able to go to sleep.'

'None of us could tonight,' said Jack. 'I've never felt so wide awake in my life. I'm going to get some clothes on first. I haven't had time to put any on. Wasn't I glad to get some rugs round me, though!'

'I'm pretty wet through myself,' said Bill. 'I'll have a few rugs too, I think.'

'There's some clothes of Horace's in that locker,' said Dinah. 'The one behind you. We gave him all of his, as we thought, but I found some more yesterday, tucked away there. They won't fit you, Bill, but at least they'll keep you warm.'

'Good,' said Bill, and opened the locker. 'I'll put them on now, if I can feel what they are in the dark. You girls get some food, if you've got any. Pity we can't boil a kettle and get something hot into us!'

Soon Bill and the boys had dry clothes on. Then all five of them sat close together for warmth, and ate biscuits and chocolate hungrily.

'Now suppose we tell each other what's happened since I so hurriedly departed from Puffin Island,' said Bill.

'You tell your tale first,' said Lucy-Ann, pressing close to him. 'Oh, Bill, it's good to have you back! I was so scared when we found you were gone, and the engine of the motor-boat smashed up, and the wireless too.'

'Yes. They told me they'd done that,' said Bill. 'Apparently they didn't know you kids were on the island at all – so I didn't say a word, of course. Well – to make a long story short, when I was fiddling about with the wireless that night, on our boat, trying to get a message through – and not succeeding, unfortunately . . .'

'Oh, Bill – then we shan't be rescued!' said Lucy-Ann at once. 'Oh, we did hope you would have sent a message for help or something! . . .'

'Well, headquarters knew that I was on to something up here, but no more than that,' said Bill. 'Anyway, as I say, I was fiddling with the wireless – when I suddenly got a blow on the head, and down I went. Then I knew nothing more at all until I woke up on some other island, a prisoner in a shack!'

'The enemy didn't hurt you, did they?' asked Lucy-Ann anxiously.

Bill didn't answer that. He went on with his tale. 'They questioned me, of course, and got nothing out of me at all.

The queer part was that the very men I'd been told to disappear from, because they were after me, were the very men we bumped into up here! *This* was where they were carrying on their activities! I had thought it was somewhere in Wales – but they made me think that by laying false clues.'

'Oh, Bill – and to think this wild desolate sea, with all its little islands, was the very place they had chosen, and *we*, too, chose to come to!' said Jack. 'They must have thought you'd found out their hiding-place, and had come to track them down.'

'Just what they did think,' said Bill. 'And what's more they imagined that one or other of their men must have given their secret away, and they wanted to find out from me who it was. That was why they held me for questioning, I imagine – instead of bumping me off at once.'

'Humpy-dumpy-bumpy,' said Kiki, taking her head out from under her wing. But nobody paid the slightest attention. Bill's story was too absorbing.

'They wanted to know *how* much I knew, and *who* had told me,' said Bill. 'Well, I didn't actually know very much, and what I did know nobody had told me, so they didn't get a great deal out of me – and they were not pleased.'

'Didn't you *really* know very much then?' said Philip, astonished.

'I knew this gang were up to something illegal – I knew they were getting a lot of money from somewhere – I guessed it was something to do with guns,' said Bill. 'I tried to put several spokes in their wheel, and they got wise to the fact that I was after them. I'd cleaned up a nasty little business of theirs once before – though we didn't get the chief ones then – so I wasn't popular.'

'And they decided to track *you* down and bump you off!' said Jack. 'So you were told to disappear – and lo and behold! you came here to disappear . . .'

'And walked right into the hornets' nest,' agreed Bill. 'And took you with me too! How is it you kids always attract adventures? As soon as I go near you, an adventure leaps up, and we all get caught in it.'

'It *is* very peculiar,' said Jack. 'Go on, Bill.'

'Well, then my guards suddenly brought Mr. Horace Tipperlong to my shack,' said Bill. 'They appeared to think that he was a pal of mine, and was up here among these islands to help me in my snooping. He was just as bewildered as I was. I couldn't make him out at all. But when we were alone, he began to tell me about you kids, and I guessed what had happened. You were absolute little demons to him, according to his story.'

'Yes, we were,' said Jack remorsefully, remembering their treatment of the puzzled and angry Horace. 'You see, we honestly thought he was one of the enemy, got up to look like a rather goofy ornithologist, sent to capture us and make us get into his boat – so . . .'

'We captured him instead, and pushed him down a hole we found, and kept him there,' said Dinah.

'And conked him on the head every time he popped up, it appears,' said Bill. 'I shouldn't have thought you were so bloodthirsty. He said even the girls took turns at hitting him.'

'*Well*!' said everyone, in shocked astonishment at such colossal untruths. 'Bill! We never hit him once!'

'I wouldn't have been surprised at the boys giving him one or two knocks, if they really thought he was one of the enemy sent to capture them,' said Bill, 'but I simply could not *imagine* the girls hitting him. He said Lucy-Ann was the worst.'

'*Oh!* And I was the only one that said I couldn't possibly,' said Lucy-Ann, really shocked at such wicked statements.

'Anyway, apparently you gave him an awful time, and then made off with his boat, leaving him to be captured by the enemy,' said Bill. 'You know, I couldn't help grinning when I heard it all. There's plenty of pluck in you kids! The enemy took him off in their boat and didn't believe a word of his story about your taking him prisoner. They really thought he was a pal of mine. Of course, I pretended not to believe his tale about there being children on the island either, because I didn't want you captured as well. But I did wonder what was happening to you when I heard you'd taken his boat. Horace said it was no longer in the little harbour when he was yanked on board the enemy's boat.'

'I don't like Horace,' said Lucy-Ann. 'I hope the enemy give him an *awful* time! He's silly and he's untruthful and he's a coward.'

'And if he hadn't yelled out when he did tonight, just after I'd opened the hatch of the cabin to let you out, Bill, we'd have been able to capture that big fast motor-boat, and get right back to the mainland,' said Jack gloomily. 'Silly idiot – yelling like that!'

'Yes, that was a great pity,' said Bill. 'Now you tell me *your* story.'

So the children told it, and Bill listened with interest and amazement. When they came to the bit about the lagoon, and what was hidden there, he held his breath in astonishment.

'So *that's* where they put the guns – dropped them by parachute into a secret lagoon – and then meant to get them up again as soon as the time was ripe – and take them away by seaplane. Gun-running on the grand scale!'

'We were jolly astonished when we watched it all happening,' said Jack.

'I should think so!' said Bill. 'It's beyond belief! And to think you children stumbled on the whole secret. My word, if only I could get a message through to headquarters, we'd catch the whole gang red-handed!'

'It's been pretty thrilling,' said Philip. 'We had some scares, I can tell you, Bill.'

'You're good kids,' said Bill. 'Good and plucky kids. I'm proud of you. But there's one thing I don't understand.

Why didn't you make for safety, when you captured Horace's boat? Why did you mess about here?'

'Well . . .' said Jack, 'you see – we had the choice of making for safety – or trying to find you. And we chose to try and find you, Bill. Even Lucy-Ann voted for that.'

There was a silence. Then Bill put his big arms all round the huddled-up four and gave them such a hug that Lucy-Ann gasped.

'I don't know what to say,' said Bill, in a queer sort of voice. 'You're only kids – but you're the finest company of friends anyone could have. You know the meaning of loyalty already, and even if you're scared you don't give up. I'm proud to have you for my friends.'

'Oh, *Bill*!' said Lucy-Ann, tremendously thrilled to hear such a speech from her hero. 'You *are* nice. You're our very very best friend, and you always will be.'

'Always,' said Dinah.

The boys said nothing, but they glowed inwardly at Bill's praise. Friendship – loyalty – staunchness in face of danger – they and Bill both knew these things and recognised them for the fine things they were. They felt very close to Bill indeed.

'Look!' said Lucy-Ann suddenly. 'The dawn! Over there, in the east. Oh, Bill – I wonder what's going to happen today?'

Chapter 29
Bill makes a grand find

The sky grew silvery in the east. Then a golden glow spread slowly upwards, and the sea became a milky colour that gradually turned to gold.

Almost at once there came a crying of seabirds as guillemots, gannets, cormorants, puffins and gulls came from their roosting-places to greet the new day. Soon the sea around the children was dotted thickly with hundreds of birds eagerly seeking fish for food. Huffin and Puffin joined them.

Jack gave an exclamation as he looked all round him. 'This isn't the lagoon-island. There were no rocky cliffs to it like this, facing the sea. This is another island we've come to!'

'Yes, it is,' said Philip. 'One I don't remember to have seen before. Blow! Where are we?'

'I should think it must be the island we once noticed on the chart,' said Lucy-Ann, remembering. 'The Isle of Wings. Just *look* at the mass of birds on the waters round us! It's more than we've ever seen before!'

'Extraordinary!' said Bill, amazed. 'There must be millions of birds. Some of them are so close that they bob against each other.'

Not only the sea was full of birds, but the air too, and the screaming and calling was deafening. Soon one bird after another flew up from the water with fish in its beak. Huffin flew to the boat and presented Philip with his usual beakful of neatly arranged fish.

'Kiki's very quiet,' said Philip, looking at her. 'What's the matter with her? Kiki, put up your crest, you ridiculous bird!'

'Send for the doctor,' said Kiki mournfully. Jack looked at her closely. Then he gave an exclamation.

'She's lost some of her crest! She's hardly got any! Oh, Bill – that's what she screeched for last night! A bullet must have zipped through her crest – right through her top-knot – and taken some of the feathers off with it.'

'Poor Polly, poor Polly, what a pity, what a pity!' said Kiki, glad to be the centre of attention.

'Yes, poor old Kiki!' said Jack, and he fondled her. 'What a shock you must have got! No wonder you screeched. Never mind, old thing – the crest will grow again. You'll look a bit mangy for a while, but *we* shan't mind.'

Bill had been looking to see exactly what had happened

to the boat. It had run on to a shelf of rock, and had settled there so firmly that until high tide came there was no hope of getting off. They were not on the mainland of the island, but on an outcrop of tall rocks, hung with thick seaweed, and inhabited by about two hundred or more birds. They did not seem to mind the boat and its load of people in the least. In fact, seeing Huffin and Puffin perched there, some of the birds came on deck too. Jack was thrilled.

'I don't think the boat's damaged at all,' said Bill. 'Once she gets afloat again with the tide, she'll be all right. But the thing is – what in the world are we going to do if she does get afloat?'

'Row to safety,' said Lucy-Ann promptly.

'Sounds easy,' said Jack scornfully. 'But you don't realise what a wild and desolate sea this is, Lucy-Ann, or how few people ever come to these little bird-islands. We couldn't possibly row to the mainland, for instance, could we, Bill?'

'No. I don't think so,' said Bill. 'I'm glad to see we've got a good store of food. That's something. But what about drinking-water?'

'We'll have to drink pineapple juice or something like that,' said Dinah. 'And if it rains we'll catch rainwater.'

'What *is* the best thing to do?' said Bill, talking to himself, with a frown. 'They'll be looking for us, I expect. They'll know we couldn't get far. They'll send out patrols – probably even an aeroplane. They can't afford to let me get away now.'

The children knew that 'they' meant the enemy. Dinah looked all round them. 'If the enemy do come round this island, they can't help seeing us. We'd be spotted at once in our boat.'

'Well – we'll make up our minds what to do when the boat's afloat again,' said Bill at last. 'What about a spot of sleep? Lucy-Ann is looking as white as a sheet. She's had no sleep at all.'

'I do feel awfully sleepy,' admitted Lucy-Ann, trying not

to yawn. 'But I feel dirty and sticky too.'

'Let's have a quick dip in the sea, and then have a snooze,' said Jack. 'We can take it in turn to keep watch for the enemy.'

'I don't want a dip,' said Dinah. 'I'm too sleepy. You three and Bill have a dip, and I'll make up our beds again and get the rugs and things set out comfortably.'

'I'll help you,' said Lucy-Ann. 'I'm too tired to bathe.'

Bill and the boys soon slipped into the water. The girls watched them. 'You know,' said Lucy-Ann, after a while, 'it's almost impossible to see the boys and Bill among all those birds bobbing about. Once I lose sight of them I can't spot them again.'

It was quite true. There were so many birds bobbing about on the water that the boys' wet dark heads, and Bill's, could hardly be picked out from the crowd.

'Let's tell Bill when they come back,' said Dinah, a sudden idea sliding into her head. 'I bet if we all slid into the water if the enemy came, nobody would ever spot us among the birds there.'

No, they wouldn't,' agreed Lucy-Ann. 'It would be a marvellous idea, Dinah!'

They told the others when they came back, glowing from their bathe. Bill nodded, pleased. 'Yes – a fine idea. If the enemy comes in sight, that's what we'll do. Our heads would be completely lost among the bodies of the swimming birds.'

'What about the boat though?' said Jack.

'We could do what we did for ourselves, when we were on the rocks beside the lagoon,' said Philip. 'Drape it with seaweed so that it looks like a rock!'

'You're full of bright ideas, you kids,' said Bill. 'Whilst you're all having a snooze I'll do a little boat-draping. If the enemy come, they'll come soon. They won't waste many hours before they try to find us. I'll wake you if I see or hear any sign of them, and you must all be prepared to drop over the side of the boat. Better sleep in your undies, so that you don't wet all your clothes. Your bathing-suits are wet.'

'Ours aren't,' said Lucy-Ann. 'Oh dear – I'm so awfully sleepy. I do hope the enemy don't come yet. I'm not at all sure I shall wake if they do!'

Bill tucked them all up in rugs. They were asleep in a moment or two, tired out. Bill began to do a little boat-draping. He pulled great fronds of seaweed off the nearby rocks and hung them over the boat-sides, till the little vessel looked like a boat-shaped rock.

Having finished his task, Bill sat down in the cabin. He idly removed a cover from something there – and then stared in surprise.

A wireless! Was it a transmitter too? Surely Horace, going off all alone into the wilds, would have had the sense to take a transmitter with him, in case he got hurt, or became ill? With trembling hands Bill began to examine the wireless.

He gave a loud exclamation that woke up Jack. The boy sat up in alarm. 'Is it the enemy, Bill?'

'No. But look here – why on earth didn't you tell me there was a wireless in this boat? I can get a message through, with luck.'

'Golly! I forgot all about it!' said Jack. 'But is it a transmitter, Bill?'

'Yes. Not a very good one – but I'll do my best to try and work it so that I can send a message to headquarters,' said Bill. 'There's always someone standing by there, hoping to hear from me. I haven't reported for days.'

Bill began to hunt about and Jack wondered why. 'What are you looking for, Bill?' he asked.

'The aerial,' said Bill. 'There must be an aerial some-where, for the transmitter. Where on earth can it be?'

'I remember seeing something on a shelf at the back of the cabin,' said Jack sleepily. 'It was about six feet long.'

'That would be it!' said Bill, and went to look. He pulled

out something long and slender. 'Good! Here it is. I can soon fix it up.'

Jack watched Bill for a few minutes, then he felt his eyes closing and he slumped down in his rugs again. It was very, very exciting to watch Bill putting up the aerial and trying to make the transmitter work – but not even that excitement could make Jack's eyes keep open. In half a second he was fast asleep again.

Bill worked and worked, groaning occasionally with disappointment as first one thing failed and then another. Curious sounds came from the wireless, and little lights glowed here and there within it. There was something the matter with it, and Bill didn't know what. If only he knew! Oh, if only he could get the thing to work, just for a minute or two!

At last he thought he had got it fixed. Now to send a message through. Now to send out his code number and wait for a reply.

He sent out his code time and again. There was no reply. The wireless seemed to be quite dead at his end. There was nothing for it but to send a message and hope it would be received – but Bill had grave doubts about it.

He rapidly sent a message through in code, asking for immediate help. He repeated the message time and time again, but got no reply at all. He gave the lagoon-island as a guide to their whereabouts, knowing that they must be somewhere near it. Surely it must be on some map, and could be located?

He was so busy trying to send his message and listening for a reply which never came, that he almost didn't hear the distant purr of a powerful motor-boat. But the sound did at last penetrate his mind and he looked up with a start.

He shouted to the children. 'Wake up! Quick! Into the water with you – the enemy are here! WAKE UP!'

They all woke up with a jump. The enemy! Splash! Into the water they slid, all five of them, the two girls hardly awake. The enemy! Yes, there was the motor-boat heading straight for them all!

Chapter 30
Ahoy there! Show yourselves!

There was a sudden flash of sunlight on the lenses of a pair of field-glasses. They were being levelled at the island, on whose rocks the children's boat had been grounded. The glasses swept the rocks and the island, and then came back to the rocks again.

The boat was there, draped end to end with seaweed. The glasses rested on it for a few moments. Then they swept the sea, but among the bobbing birds it was impossible to pick out the five wet heads.

The children kept as close to swimming birds as possible. Philip was all right because Huffin and Puffin perched on his head, and hid him beautifully. Lucy-Ann was near a big cormorant, who eyed her with interest but did not swim away from her. Dinah and Jack were among a crowd of bobbing, diving puffins, and Bill, fearful of his big, somewhat bald head being spotted, kept bobbing under the water, and holding his breath there as long as he could.

After what seemed an age the enemy's motor-boat swung round and went away, going right round the island – or so Bill thought. They heard the sound of its engine growing fainter and fainter.

Not until it had completely died away did Bill let the children get back into the boat. Then, when he thought it was quite safe, they all clambered back, wet and hungry, but no longer sleepy.

'How slippery the boat is, with all this seaweed!' said Jack. 'Dinah, your idea worked well. I don't think the enemy even *guessed* there was anyone here – and there were five people and a boat within easy sight of their glasses.'

'Yes, a very fine idea, Dinah,' said Bill. 'Now – what about breakfast? I'm starving!'

They sat down and opened a few tins. Kiki screeched with delight when she saw the chunks of pineapple in one of them. She tried to raise her crest, but as she had only one or two feathers left in it, it was not a very successful effort.

Jack suddenly thought of something. 'Bill! Do I remember something – something about you and Horace's wireless – or did I dream it? Yes, perhaps I dreamt it.'

'You certainly didn't,' said Bill. 'I found Horace's wireless – most unexpectedly, I must say – and discovered to my joy that it was a transmitter as well as a receiver – so that I ought to be able to send messages as well as receive them.'

'Oh, *Bill*! So you've wirelessed for help – and we shall be saved!' said Lucy-Ann joyfully.

'Unfortunately there's something wrong with the thing,' said Bill. 'Couldn't get a chirp out of it – and whether or not my messages have gone through I can't tell. But probably not. It's not a very good set, this one of Horace's.'

'Oh – so it's not very likely it was of much use,' said Dinah, disappointed.

'Not very,' said Bill. 'By the way, did anyone feel a slight upward lift then? I have an idea the boat is coming off the rocks.'

He was right. It was soon afloat, and Bill took the oars. He rowed for some distance away from the island, and then a thought struck him.

'Look here – Horace couldn't possibly have come all the way up here – and hoped to get back again – without a store of petrol. Have you examined this boat thoroughly?'

'No, not really thoroughly,' said Jack. 'It isn't much of a boat.'

'I grant you that – but there really *should* be some petrol somewhere,' said Bill. 'Philip, pull up those piles of rope and stuff. There would be room under the boards there for tins of petrol.'

Philip and Jack did as they were told. They hauled up three loose boards – and there, neatly arranged below, was Horace's store of petrol!

'Gosh!' said Jack. 'What a find! *Now* we'll be all right. We'll be on the mainland in no time. Good old Horace!'

They handed Bill a tin. He emptied it into the petrol tank of the engine and then took another tin. That was emptied in too. Hurrah! Now they could really make headway.

Soon the engine was purring happily away and the little boat was speeding over the waves. No more rowing! Bill set his course for the south-east.

'Hark! There's an aeroplane about somewhere!' said Lucy-Ann suddenly. 'I can hear it.'

They all looked up into the sky. Soon they saw the plane, coming from the north-east. It was flying low.

'Looks as if it's trying to spot us,' said Bill uneasily.

'It belongs to the enemy then!' said Jack. They all looked intently at the approaching plane. It seemed suddenly to see them, and veered in their direction. It flew down very low, circled round them, and then made off.

'Blow!' said Bill. 'Now we're for it! They'll send out their most powerful motor-boat – or maybe one of the seaplanes they seem to use – and that'll be that!'

'Well, we've got plenty of petrol,' said Jack, 'so we can keep on quickly for miles. We'll be well away from here before long.'

The boat sped on, Bill giving her her top speed. When he reckoned that her petrol would soon be running out he called to Jack, 'Get out the other tins, Jack. I'll put some more in before she's empty.'

But what a shock for the boys! All the other tins were empty! Bill stared in dismay.

'Gosh! Somebody has swindled Horace properly! He probably gave orders for all the tins to be filled – and somebody took the money for the lot, and only filled half. What a dirty trick!'

'But just the sort that *would* be played on poor silly Horace!' said Philip. 'Oh, Bill – we're out on the open sea now, miles away from any island. What will we do if the petrol gives out before we've reached anywhere?'

Bill wiped his forehead. 'I don't like this,' he said. 'There's not much left in the tank now. Once we run out, we can't get far with oars, and we shall be at the mercy of any fast motor-boat sent out to catch us. I think perhaps one of the bullets must have glanced off the petrol tank and made it leak a bit.'

Nobody said anything. 'Oh dear,' thought Lucy-Ann,

'just as we think things are all right, they turn out all wrong again.'

After a while the engine stopped with a series of coughs and splutters. 'No more petrol,' said Jack gloomily.

'Send for the doctor,' said Kiki.

'Wish we could,' said Philip.

'Arrrrrr!' said Huffin from the deck-rail. Both Huffin and Puffin were still with the little company. Lucy-Ann had begun to hope that they would travel right home with them. What excitement they would cause!

'This is really disgusting,' said Bill. 'So near and yet so far!'

There was a dead silence, and only the plish-plash of the sea against the sides of the boat could be heard. Philip's rats, surprised at the quiet, ran out of their various hiding-places in his clothes, and sniffed the air. Bill hadn't seen them since he had been captured from Puffin Island, and he stared in surprise.

'My word – how they've grown! Well, well, who knows, we may have to eat them in the end!'

He meant this as a joke, but both Lucy-Ann and Dinah took it seriously, and squealed in horror.

'Ugh! Bill! How could you say such a horrible thing! Eat a *rat*! I'd rather die!'

'Shall we row, just for something to do?' said Jack. 'Or have a meal? Or what?'

'Oh, have a meal,' said Philip. Then a thought struck him. 'I say, Bill – I suppose we oughtn't to start rationing ourselves, ought we? I mean – do you think we may be marooned out here on this lonely sea for days on end?'

'No,' said Bill, who privately thought that before the day was up they would all be back on the island in the hands of the enemy, now that their plane had spotted them. 'No. We really don't need to think of things like that at the moment. All the same – I wouldn't have headed out for the open sea as we have done, if I'd thought the petrol was going to give out – I'd have kept near the islands.'

It was a boring and anxious day. The four children were still very tired, but refused to try and sleep. No motor-boat appeared in chase of them. The sun began to sink in the west, and it looked as if the little company was going to spend a night out on the open sea.

'Well, thank goodness it isn't cold, anyway,' said Dinah. 'Even the wind is warm tonight. Don't we seem a long long way from home – and from school – and from all the ordinary things we know?'

Lucy-Ann gazed round her at the vast open sea, green near the boat, but a deep blue beyond. 'Yes,' she said, 'we're far away from everywhere – lost on the Sea of Adventure.'

The sun slid down further still. Then, on the evening air, came a familiar sound – the throb-throb-throb of a powerful engine.

Everyone sat up straight at once. Motor-boat? Aeroplane? Seaplane? What was it?

'There it is!' cried Jack, making everyone jump. 'Look, over there! Golly, what a big one! It's a seaplane.'

'It must be the one we saw on the lagoon the other day,' said Dinah. 'They've sent it after us. Oh, Bill – what can we do?'

'All lie down flat,' said Bill at once. 'You've got to remember that if it's the enemy they don't know I've got children with me – they probably think there are three or four men in the boat – and they may shoot, as they did before. So lie down flat and don't move. Don't show your heads at all.'

Lucy-Ann's knees began their familiar wobbly feeling. She lay down flat at once, glad that Bill had not suggested that the boys should squash on top of them again. Bill put his arm over her.

'Don't you worry, Lucy-Ann,' he said. 'You'll be all right. They won't hurt children.'

But Lucy-Ann didn't want 'them' to hurt Bill either, and she was very much afraid they would. With her pale face pressed into the rugs, she lay as still as a mouse.

The roar of the seaplane came much nearer. It circled just overhead. Then its engine cut out and it landed not far off. Waves from it rippled under the boat and sent it up and down.

Nobody dared to look overboard and see the great seaplane. Bill was afraid of a bullet if he did.

Then a colossal voice came booming over the sea, the voice of a giant: 'AHOY THERE! SHOW YOURSELVES!'

'Don't move,' said Bill urgently. 'Don't move. Don't be frightened, Lucy-Ann. They're using a megaphone, that's why the voice sounds so loud.'

The giant voice came again: 'WE'VE GOT OUR GUNS ON YOU. ANY FUNNY BUSINESS AND YOU'LL BE BLOWN TO SMITHEREENS. SHOW YOURSELVES!'

Chapter 31
Over the sea of adventure

'It's no good,' said Bill, in a low voice. 'I must stand up. I don't want them to machine-gun the boat.'

He stood up and waved, then put both hands up to show that he surrendered. A boat put off from the seaplane and came rapidly towards Bill's boat. In it were three men, one of them holding a revolver in his hand.

The children waited, panic-stricken, fearing to hear a shot at Bill. They had none of them raised their heads, but they could picture all too plainly what was happening.

The boat came near – and then there came a loud cry of amazement from it.

'BILL! By all that's wonderful, it's BILL! Why on earth didn't you welcome us, instead of making us think you were part of the gang!'

'Good heavens! It's you, Joe!' yelled Bill, and the relief in his voice brought all the children to their feet at once. 'Look here, kids – it's Joe – my colleague. Hey, Joe, you got my message then, all right?'

The boat came alongside with a gentle bump. Joe put away his revolver, grinning. 'Yes, I got your wireless message all right – but I guess you didn't get ours. We kept asking you questions, and all you did was to go on repeating the same old thing. So this seaplane was sent out and we were just cruising along looking for the lagoon you told us about, when we spotted your boat here. So down we came to investigate.'

'Thank goodness,' said Bill. 'We'd run out of petrol. We were expecting the enemy to send a plane or a boat out after us at any moment!'

'Come along to the seaplane,' said Joe, who had bright-blue eyes and a very wide grin. 'Will the kids mind flying?'

'Oh no. We're used to it,' said Jack, and helped the girls into the boat where Joe stood.

'Are we rescued?' said Lucy-Ann, hardly believing it could be true, after all their alarms and fears.

'You are,' said Joe, and grinned at her. 'Sent one of our biggest seaplanes after you, to take you home! Have to do that for Bill here, you know. He's a V.I.P.'

'What's that?' asked Lucy-Ann, as they sped towards the seaplane.

'Very Important Person, of course,' said Joe. 'Didn't you know he was?'

'Yes,' said Lucy-Ann, beaming. 'Oh yes. I always knew he was.'

'We've left Huffin and Puffin behind,' suddenly wailed Dinah.

'Good heavens! Was there somebody else in your boat then?' said Joe in alarm. 'Never saw them!'

'Oh, they're only puffins,' said Jack. 'But awfully nice ones, quite tame. Oh, there they are, flying after the boat.'

'Can we take them with us?' begged Lucy-Ann. But Bill shook his head.

'No, Lucy-Ann. They'd be miserable away from their home here in the islands. Soon they will nest again and lay an egg. Then they will forget all about us.'

'I shall never, never forget them,' said Lucy-Ann. 'They kept with us all the time!'

'Here we are,' said Joe, as they came to the enormous seaplane. They were helped into it, and then the plane took off smoothly and sweetly, circling into the air like a broad-winged gull. Horace's boat was left bobbing alone, waiting for one of the police boats to collect it.

'What about that lagoon?' said Joe suddenly. 'I'd like to spot it, and plot it on our maps. I think we can find it. Will these kids know it if they see it?'

'Oh *yes*,' said Jack. 'You can't mistake it. It's a most extraordinary sea-lake, and much bluer than the sea. I shouldn't be surprised if you can see some of the packages under the water, if you go down low. The water's so clear there.'

The seaplane roared through the sky. The children were thrilled. Down below was the blue sea, looking smooth and still. Then, as they looked, they saw little islands coming into view. What hosts of them there were!

Then Jack caught sight of the lagoon. 'There it is, there it is!' he shouted. 'Look down there! You can't mistake it, lying between those two islands, shut in by a reef of rocks all the way round.'

The seaplane circled round the surprising lagoon. It dropped lower. The children watched to see if they could make out any of the underwater packages – and sure enough, through the clear water glimmered the silvery-grey wrappings that covered the hidden guns.

'That's where the guns are,' said Philip. 'Look, Bill – you can see the waterproof wrappings! They had already begun to lift the packages from the water and load them on to seaplanes. We watched them loading one.'

Bill and Joe exchanged glances. 'We've got some pretty good witnesses then,' said Joe. 'Good bunch of kids, this, Bill. Are they the ones you've gone adventuring with before?'

'They are,' said Bill. 'You can't keep them out of adventures, you know. And they will drag me into them too!'

They left the lagoon with its sinister secret behind them and flew over the island where Bill had been a prisoner. 'There's the little jetty,' said Jack, as they flew low. 'And look, there are *two* motor-boats there now! I say, Bill – what about Horace?'

'Horace will be rescued when we clean up these scoundrels,' said Bill. 'They're the men who make fortunes when one country goes to war with another, or when civil war is fought – because they get the guns and sell them to each side. We try to stop it by all kinds of international treaties – but these men are against the law, and scorn it. That's where I come in – to stop them!'

'How will you stop them now?' asked Jack. 'Will you raid the island – and capture the men? And destroy all the hidden guns? Suppose they escape by motor-boat or plane?'

'Don't you worry about that,' said Joe, with his wide grin stretching across his brown face. 'We've got messages through already. There'll be a fleet of our seaplanes up here in a few hours – and armed boats patrolling all round. There's no hope for any of the gang now.'

Except for the little jetty, which would hardly have been noticed if the children and Bill hadn't known it was there, there was nothing to see on the enemy's island at all.

'Everything well camouflaged,' said Bill. 'A clever lot, and I've been after them for a long time. They sent me off on all kinds of false trails and I'd almost given up hope of finding their lair. But there it is.'

'They *must* have been surprised to see you up here, Bill!' said Lucy-Ann, as the seaplane left the enemy's island behind.

'Oh, look – there's the island where we landed with Bill!'

cried Dinah. 'Puffin Island! Do look! There's the bird-cliff – and you can just see the little narrow channel going into the cliff – only you have to look hard to see it. And there's where we had our signal fire.'

'And there's where we had our tents that blew away in the storm – by those few trees,' said Jack. 'And look, there's the puffin colony!'

The seaplane flew down as low as it dared. It flew low enough for the children to see a moving mass of birds, scared of the enormous noise made by the seaplane's powerful engines.

'I can see Huffin and Puffin!' cried Lucy-Ann. The others roared with laughter.

'You can't, you fibber!' said Dinah.

'No, I can't really. I'm pretending to,' said Lucy-Ann. 'I want them to be there always. I want them to have their own burrow, and a nest – and an egg! I want them to have a lovely baby puffin that would be tame too. Goodbye, dear Huffin and Puffin! We did so love having you for pets.'

'Arrrrrrrr!' suddenly said Kiki, for all the world as if she understood what Lucy-Ann was saying.

'Kiki's saying "good-bye" in puffin language,' said Lucy-Ann. 'Arrrrr, Huffin and Puffin! I'm saying good-bye too.'

And from the scared puffin colony rose a medley of deep guttural *arrrrrrrs* as the birds settled down once more. Those that had run down burrows popped up again and added their *arrrrr* to the chorus.

'What a lot we shall have to tell Mother,' said Philip. 'I wonder how she is?'

Joe smiled at him. 'Getting on fine, except for worrying about you four,' he said. 'She'll feel better still when she gets our wireless message.'

'Oh, have you sent one already?' asked Dinah. 'Oh, good! Now she'll know we're all right. Goodness – won't it be queer to go back to school after all this?'

School! Sitting at a desk, learning French grammar, getting into rows for leaving tennis racquets about, playing silly tricks, having music lessons, going to bed at the proper time – how very, very queer it would all seem!

Only Lucy-Ann thought of it with real pleasure. 'It'll be so nice to wake up in the mornings and know there's only lessons and tennis and things to worry about,' she said to Bill. 'Instead of wondering if the enemy is coming, and seeing planes parachuting guns down into lagoons, and rushing about in motor-boats, and . . .'

'Conking poor Horace on the head,' said Bill, grinning.

'Well, we *didn't* do that, whatever he said to you,' said Lucy-Ann. 'And if ever I see him again I'm going to tell him I'm sorry we made such an awful mistake – but that honestly he deserves a good old – a good old . . .'

'Conk,' said Philip, chuckling.

'Well, conk if you like,' said Lucy-Ann. 'A good old conk for telling such awful stories.'

The seaplane was flying south now. It had left behind all the exciting little islands, and all the millions of noisy sea-birds. The sun was now almost gone and the sea was shadowed a deep blue. In a few minutes the first stars would prick through the evening sky, as bright as diamonds.

'We'll be over the mainland soon,' said Bill. 'Thank goodness it's all ended up well! I thought it was the finish of everything when this seaplane landed beside us and hailed us. Another adventure to talk over when we see each other in the holidays. What a lot we've had together!'

'I think I've liked this one the best,' said Jack thoughtfully, and he scratched what was left of Kiki's crest. 'All those islands – and this lonely sea, with its blues and greens and greys.'

'The Sea of Adventure,' said Lucy-Ann, looking down at its vast expanse of dark blue, touched here and there with the golden reflection of the sky. 'Good-bye, Sea of Adventure! You're a lovely place – but *much* too exciting for me!'